***

—

THE OTHER BLUE

FROM THE MAN WHO DIDN'T STOP RUNNING SERIES

BY BRIAN JAMES

RED Publishing Baltimore, MD 21231

ISBN: 9798366041911

Printed in the United States of America.

First, I thank God for life, love, health, and family. To my parents, thank you for being my light. To my little brother, Justin, you are the gift that I am thankful for each day. To my lovely lady, Ashley, thank you for remaining by my side. To my therapist, "Super Vicky", you've introduced me to healing by introducing me to myself. Thank you for saving my life.

I've got quite the village and far too many names to list but, to other family and friends who have supported me through it all, thank you.

In loving memory of Gordon G. Everett, Sr.

CONTENTS

INTRODUCTION

Professor Rose beat his alarms today. His teeth practically brushed themselves. He had showered the night before and for the first time in 27 years, he didn't care about what he was wearing. All he could think about on the train downtown was his fourth session with the honorable Austin Arrington.

His colleagues at Impact were jealous of the opportunity. Not the angry type of jealousy but the kind that gets you a pat on the back in the break room. Everyone knew that Austin was going to do a sit down with one of his rising psychiatrists. Everyone hoped that it would be them. It's nearly impossible to squeeze all of his accomplishments into just one week of interviews but he didn't have much choice. It was the perfect, and only, time to tell the story of the man who didn't stop running.

We just heard the tale of Paradise in our last meeting between Rose and Arrington. He hadn't even started telling the story behind ImpactComm, yet. We found out how he met his mentor and friend, Derry Miercone'. His wisdom became one of the strongest voices in Arrington's journey and we got to see his life change ever since meeting him. Yesterday was more about Arrington's transition from basketball to media. It was about sacrifice and how important it is to understanding love. It was also about the high society that orchestrates the media, entertainment, and other major industries. A hive of mega-billionaires who make the world turn while the rest of us spend our days on the hamster wheels – lining their pockets.

Austin had to experience Paradise because it would set up his place at the table. It happens to us all as we climb the ladder in our passion. We meet new devils on the way up. That's part of why Austin wanted to share this story before his time was up. His life can teach others how to love but it also shares his secrets to success in business and how he dealt with the many devils he met on the way up the ladder.

That story continues as Professor Rose sits with Austin for the fourth of five sessions. We're getting into one of the most exciting times of Austin's family-life and a pivotal moment in his investment into ImpactComm. These are the moments that built up his company. Its foundation. The libraries, laboratories, technology, science facilities, and entertainment centers wouldn't be what they are if it weren't for what Austin Arrington is going to share with Professor Rose, today.

This is another tale about the man who didn't stop running.

PROLOGUE

He was waiting for me today. We were both excited to see each other. Something about his sharing of the Paradise story brought us closer. He didn't fight me anymore. At least not today. Mr. Arrington was dressed rather nicely. A much more stylish ensemble than that god-awful hospital gown. It was a very nice turtleneck sweater with gray slacks and slippers. Reminiscent of those earlier days of his career; he looked like he was going in for a day at the office. Well, minus the slippers.

Our conversation yesterday was a lot for me to process so I appreciated his sharing.

"He's been talking about you all morning," the pretty nurse from Tallahassee told me as I checked-in. "Up early and everything."

I nodded and smiled. Her eyes pointed to his room and he was standing in the doorway; stoic, cheery, tall, and open. It felt like one of those days that could have been painted on a postcard. Golden hallways, sun-kissed window panes, and a successful black entrepreneur willing to share his secrets. I smirked at him and nodded like Monday morning. I was pinching myself on the inside. I wanted to make sure I wasn't dreaming.

"Come'on! Come! Sir," another nurse led me from around the nurse's station. She was practically skipping down the hall.

We got to his room and he didn't say a word. His smile was loud.

> "Ok," the nurse clenched like a magician before the end of the show, "surprise!" She slid out of the way like she was on stage with the Supremes. "We didn't know your, uh, favorite so we just grabbed a little bit of everything," she continued. "Mr. Arrington asked if we could do something special today and well, we loved it. He just wouldn't stop smiling-"

She wasn't lying – he still hadn't said a word. Just standing there with the smile of a Sunday morning in Florida. The pretty nurse walked in and massaged Mr. Arrington's shoulders like a proud daughter would. They were waiting for me to grab a plate and I definitely didn't mind doing so. There was enough coffee in there to wake up every surgeon on the east coast. It was great. It felt good to chat with the nurses and the esteemed Austin Arrington. He was always as humble as advertised. I learned a lot that morning – about service, joy, and pure love.

The french toast had been devoured and the coffee had got into our systems. Now it was time for us to have our fourth session. The nurses left the room as it was and closed the door in silence. As careful as a dentist in the eleventh hour of a root canal. He stared at me with a smile. I took my seat and opened my notebook.

> He said, "today, you're going to learn some good stuff, son."

These are his words from our session.

1 HELLA GOOD

I was staring at the aluminum imagining what life was like on the other side. My mind was as busy as Times Square. It felt like a battle between my voices of reason, defending their sides of the aisle.

We were spaced out and it was only 8 of us. There was plenty of room to breathe even though a small part of me wanted to suffocate. She was sitting toward the rear, her dress was red and ripe. You never imagine yourself falling from the sky until you actually are. The uncertainty whisking by, as vast as the horizon stretches. But, Sia smiled in that red dress. We'd become more than friends by then. Her finger flicked the lighter to her cigarette. I heard it echo over the engines. The smile she dressed herself with was enough to keep me warm. It always was. We were living on a high from Paradise. The Honeymoon was perfectly imperfect enough to never slip my mind. The good and the bad. She taught me many things on that trip and I still feed from her bosom months later.

Is that oil I smell? Is that safe? At this point, it's probably safer to ignore the risks. They may cause an aneurysm or heart failure. Better to just pretend that I'm a leaf falling from the sky, waiting for the ground to gently welcome me home. I'm just a bee chasing his nectar. Oh, the roses, how they balance me so well.

I kept peaking my head out of that window. You probably could guess who I was looking for. From this height though, everyone is nothing. Just one big speck of nothing in the middle of a masterpiece. All of those emotions, arguments, smiles, fears; downsized to half of a watercolor, sliding down the world's throat. Everything matters and then it doesn't.

But, then it does again.

She was still staring at me with that grin holding her stick. That same look she'd been giving me for months. It's a look with its own language. A talking-eyes type of thing, if you can imagine that. You don't have to grab your diary or open your phone, but I want you to take note of something. Take a deep breath, if you will. Imagine everything that's important to you floating just a few feet away from your clutch. The love that you've chased. Those unforgettable moments. Even those unfortunate events that somehow started dancing and made you who you are today. You've found a way to love it all and now they live as slaves to time and strangers to gravity. Can you see them floating around you? Losing color as the sand slides through the hourglass?

***

Her look reminds me of that reality. It always has. She uses those eyes to say *reach out and grab love* or, *hold on to love*. The fearless reminder of time's power and that no matter how many flips and turns you may have to do, you should always grab onto your treasure. It's always worth fighting life's gravity for the things and the ones that you love. Never forget that. I've prayed on that for decades.

"Hey, congrats kid," Jebbs turned to me. His salt n' pepper beard was sleeping peacefully on his grungy face. "Find out where your enemy is. Get at him as soon as you can."

Well, that was weird.

"He's not going to war, dipshit," Jake said.

He was the wiry and pale guy being swallowed by the seat across from me. I could tell they had one of those weird relationships where they're the best of friends but were as different as two sides of a dirty penny.

"But congrats," he yelled over the engines. "In a few minutes, that door is'gonna open and it's just you and me, kid."

Dipshit, I mean, Jebbs was tightening some buckles on my vest while Jake was finishing his dramatic sentence. I think the antics were reasonable. Clearly there were a lot of risks in what we were doing but these two were quite an intense pair. It was exciting but I was nervous. Sweat slid into my eyelids. I think my fear was trying to hide from me.

"Remember to take it all in and she'll give it all back," Jebbs said.

I was with those two, but I was really with the lady in red. She stood up and began to dance slowly with her lips mashing that cigarette. I saw her as a red lotus, mesmerizing and graceful. Her grin felt like the antagonist to an otherwise perfect moment.

The others were tightening their buckles and making all sorts of ruckus. You would have thought we were about to drop into Normandy. It was just really-, really intense, you know? One guy was sitting right in front of the red lotus (who is still up and dancing, not a care in the world) and kept whistling some depressing tune. It wasn't as somber as 'Taps' but the two could have been cousins. It was synchronized with the lotus' movements. The cabin became some sort of melancholy circus. Oh, and intense. I promise I won't use that word anymore.

"Shit," the pilot yelled from the cockpit, which felt like miles away. Part of me wanted to yell back but the other part of me just wanted to yell. "Jake! Get your ass up here, buddy," he continued.

Nope. I can't remember his name but I remember his voice. That pilot. It was the kind that sounded like he's burned every single piece of food he's ever had in his life. Or, like his favorite pastime was drinking scorching hot coffee as a chaser to his gin -- of course, he drank his straight. Jake got up and stumbled his way to the cockpit. He disappeared as he twisted and turned through the cabin. It was silent but the whistling man and the red lotus were still giving their show. The rest of us were being human and sitting in silence because we knew something was wrong.

"Looks like we overshot the DZ, kid," Jake said walking back into the cabin.

This exciting night in me and Deja's life together all of sudden felt threatened. Like it wouldn't happen. I could already imagine the corners of her mouth anchoring into her chin, and her eyes drooping in sorrow, as we walked back onto the tarmac.

"You've got options," Jake affirmed, "we jump in the next 30 seconds and try to make our way back, or try to get clearance for a circle-around. Which we may or may not get."

Choices were never friends of mine but we'd developed a working relationship by then. I looked towards the rear of the cabin and the red lotus had stopped dancing. The other guy had stopped his somber whistling. In fact, it felt like everything had slowed. The red lotus inhaled that cigarette so deep, I know it blackened her lungs to a crisp. She closed her eyes and let the smoke serenade her exhaust system, if you will. Her head was leaned back and out of her right eye she said, "go." At least, that's what I heard. It was an ancient tongue and it also was the first time I had ever heard her voice. For months, I had just been hearing the bangles from her locs. A chilling sound.

Jake broke my daze, "kid?"

He knelt in front of me with his helmet unbuckled. There was one strap that was distracting me as it shook from the turbulence.

"Let's do it," I responded, "this moment is about Deja. 'Gotta hold it down for my lady.'"

The red lotus started dancing again as the whistling continued. Imagine her bangles playing the drums as that one guy kept whistling the cousin to *Taps*. The alarm blared and the circus was in full swing. Jake took care of that distracting buckle and began gathering things around the cabin. Dipshit and the others were gearing up, a scene that wasn't artistic at all. I knew they had done this millions of times before, but it just didn't look like it that night. The most poised of the bunch was whistling-man and Jake (he was like a real-life 'G.I Joe' type, just a little older). I want to describe the alarm to you but the best word I could think of is annoying.

It wasn't cloudy, hazy, or anything like that. Just another crisp night over Echodale. The kind you dream of when you haven't seen the stars in a while. Truth be told, I was carrying a lot of weight at that time. The (clear) night sky was the place I would rest my troubles to prepare for whatever tomorrow may bring. Work was pressure, home-life was pressure, and my social life started to feel like I was being carried upstream by the violent currents of river rafting. Without the raft, of course. The kind that makes you think you could die at any moment. At least I'd die smiling, I guess. Can't say if it would be an authentic one or not. Haven't decided yet.

"Divers stand," the pilot announced in a robotic voice, "DZ, negative five."

The intercom was ancient. It sounded gritty and muffled, like this cheap amplifier my parents bought me and Devin for Christmas '98. That was the moment when I was officially ready to get off the plane. I was pretty sure that bird was a little outdated. The things we do for our loved ones. Happy wife, happy life, right?

"Diver's door," continued the robotic pilot.

It was so dramatic and I felt like a lifeless doll going with the flow of it all.

"This is going to be uncomfortable," assured Jake.

Whenever someone says that, you have no choice but to feel weird. Doctors always said that before those preschool immunizations. The dentist said it before yanking my wisdom tooth to the heavens. That phrase never preceded comfort and Jake was right. It was very uncomfortable. *But, happy wife, happy life.*

"What'd ya say, kid?" Jake yelled through the wind.

"Happy wife, happy life," I yelled back.

He was strapped to my backside. I mean, basically inside my skin at this point. We were fourth in line for the jump. The door slid open and there was a red light oscillating just above it. I looked back to try and find the red lotus. I used to hate seeing her and now I can't stand to be without her. These eyes found comfort in it. She wasn't dancing anymore (the whistling had stopped too). Her cigarette had reached its deathbed and she was helping it kick the can, if you will. The plane shook and I lost eye contact for a second.

"DZ, negative ten. Critical," the pilot said. Jake yelled up to the front of the line (and into my left ear which is still ringing), "what are you waiting for? Now, or never, Bingo!"

That 'Bingo' guy was my favorite. You'll see why later. His nickname was fitting because he looked like a small and innocent Beagle who should have been named *Bingo*. He was the smartest and quietest of the bunch. I knew he was a tad bit crazy though because when Jake told him to jump, he turned and made a sadistic face before leaping into the sky. Within seconds, we were third in line. Then, we were next. I looked through the wind to find the red lotus, the cabin became as violent as that storm in the Wizard of Oz. At least it felt like it. My eyes cut through the whistling wind looking towards the back of the plane and then I felt a tap on my right shoulder. It was *her*. She smiled but I didn't have time to process it all. We were vacuumed into the atmosphere and it felt like my face, skin, and organs were left on the platform. Jake didn't even warn me. We laughed about that right up until his passing in 2030. It was just us and the stars, flying through the sky.

> "Stiffen your body as best as you can. I'll make it as quick as possible so you can enjoy a little bit of the show," Jake said through the wind.

I did what he asked even though I didn't really understand it. I knew that we had missed the landing site, though. It felt impossible and violent. I appreciate your concern but you must realize that I'm still here, telling you about it. What they've said about living through challenges and being able to tell the story of them, is true. There's joy in testimony.

Jake was spewing out all sorts of military-esque jargon. I tried to keep up at first but I just gave up and let him drive. He said 'stay stiff' so that's what I did and we cut through the sky like the thinnest of blades. We were all flying through the sky, actually. Everyone was so focused on the task at hand. I was worried that this band of idiots wasn't worth the coin but once we jumped out of that plane, I saw why the country paid them for what they did. I could tell that they had earned every badge of honor they had been given. It took a few seconds to process what I was hearing but the sounds of Pop Rock faded into my ears. I had on Deja's favorite earrings, a birthday gift, and they vibrated from the bass. It was drawing closer and closer as we continued to fly through the sky. My heart was pounding with the bass as it got loud. You won't believe what happened next.

I looked to my right, trying to follow the music. The wind was beating up my eyes and the tears were falling, begging for mercy. It was the red lotus and she was holding one of those vintage boomboxes above her head. She smiled as the music rumbled but I didn't know what she was so happy about. I felt like she should have been worried because, well, she didn't have a parachute. Just a boombox. I squinted (partly because the wind was kicking my eye's ass) to make sense of it all.

"Kid, we're here," Jake yelled into my daze, "look up, kid! We made it. This is the moment."

He said look up and I looked down, first. I wanted to be sure that we were really where we needed to be. I had hyped this moment up for weeks on the radio and ever since I mentioned it to Deja, her and her friends have been so excited. Paradise had introduced me to the importance of detail and by then I had begun mastering it. You see, failure was not an option for this moment. So yeah, I looked down first. I saw the mass of people standing by Lux Field and another group standing in the actual landing zone. It was well-lit with spotlights, like the ones you see outside of the club. There were LED-lit targets to give Jake and his band of idiots navigation to land. I couldn't see Deja but I knew that she could see me. I felt relieved that it had all worked out. Jake started laughing. Imagine a goblin giggling, or that one banshee sound that used to play in Scooby Doo episodes. This was that.

"Congratulations, kid," he yelled into my ear.

We halted like a dog reaching the end of his leash. The ground was just a few hundred feet away. I looked up and saw a baby blue parachute. We were having a boy.

2 VETERANS IN THE BATHROOM

Boys are fun. The manhood part worried me. That term has been tangled, twisted, and dressed so many different ways, oftentimes I don't know what the hell I'm doing. I didn't have much time to prepare for it either since we waited until the eleventh hour for the gender reveal..

When I was staring up at that blue parachute, with one of those hideous grins, all I heard were questions. *How will I keep this man alive? How will I survive this? Am I the best example for another man? What is man?* I know what you're thinking but yes, all of those questions came rushing into my mind that instant. They weren't even separate statements. It felt like one big thought. As chaotic as you can imagine.

We heard a laugh, "Ah-hah!"

It was Bingo crashing into the landing zone. He was tumbling like a basketball rolling down a hill. Except, there was no hill. At least I hoped there wasn't one. Never could be sure with that band of idiots.

"Oh, Bingo. I love that guy," Jake said, "guy's been that way for years. He's consistent for sure."

I was so giddy, I can't even tell you what I said back to him. I just remember the faint sounds of the crowd as we were getting closer to the landing zone, and how my ears were trying to find Deja's voice. Now, they did that on their own. It's like, once you fall so deep in love with someone, your body kind of lives its own life. I've told you that before and I mean it. I hope you've experienced it yourself.

The others landed much safer than our friend Bingo. We glided right into our target, feet first, damn-near perfect. The crowd was bigger than I anticipated but that was great because they all witnessed that beautiful landing. We could've charged admission for it. We jogged right out of the landing zone giving our best Tom Cruise impression (you know that 'action movie trot' right after the main character does something badass). This will be the last thing I say about the landing and then I'll move on; my favorite part was the sound of our boots hitting the ground. The boots and the buckles. I mean, we really killed it. The blue parachute dragged across the ground like a princess' gown before midnight.

Jake finally set me free (yes, we did all of that while still being strapped together -- ok, no more) and I went looking for my wife. I couldn't wait to see her smile and celebrate the moment. I imagined what the air around her tasted like. I wondered if she was wearing the red and white sweatsuit or that black dress. It was New York-chilly so my imagination was limited. Then, I saw her and couldn't have cared less what she had on. The glow did exactly what it was supposed to do. But, it was her clouds that really caught my attention. She was hunched over crying in Essence's clutch. I mean, you could see the tears dripping onto the field. Like someone was pouring water. Essence just had a kid herself so that glow was still there. Not like my Deja though.

She looked up at me with smiling eyes, "she's fine. She's fine. You know your wife."

I said something sarcastic back to her but that's just our relationship. Essence is one of my favorite characters in Deja's story. What a girl.

***

The only thing worse than a crying wife is a crying wife trying to talk -- and then, trying your hardest to understand her. You know how much of a people-pleaser I've been so you can imagine the pain of not being able to understand someone. Especially your crying wife. They were tears of joy though, I could feel them. It hurt to jog over there, dragging that heavy blue parachute, watching Deja drown. She was just a girl who was becoming a mother for the first time, crying in front of a few hundred people.

She mumbled into my arms, "ari cabinet void."

"What?"

She whined louder, "are we having a boy?"

God, it was so dramatic but I loved every bit of the antics. It was one of those rare moments that was worth the drama. Like a really good Denzel Washington film, the life changing ones. I smiled at my bride with every jewel in my soul; the rubies, the diamonds, and of course the pot of gold. I chuckled. Good thing I did because it was contagious. A laugh that we very much needed. We were so damn happy.

"Lefthand, lefthand," Derry's voice screamed closer. It had a hint of haste but no worry, or anything like that. "May I suggest, lefthand? Get your own parachute next time. What you did there, I mean,..

It- it was ok. Really, it was ok. Could have been better, but ok."

From the big straw hat to the white overcoat, I was happy to see him. Always am. Deja was happy as well. With one hand, he leaned his body up against his oak walking stick and with the other, he wrapped Deja into his arms. I think it was his own way of blessing the baby and I found it comforting as well.

"This is quite the blessing," he affirmed into Deja's eyes.

"I'm here, sir," a broken voice snuck into the atmosphere.

It was my intern, DJ. She was a compact and timid girl from the big city who would go on to be one of the most successful record executives in history. Maybe you've heard of her, DJ Peterson (goes by her married name sometime; DJ Peterson-Lake). Anyways, she started with me and Duke at RUMBLE 93.7. DJ was a very detailed person. Very trustworthy and reliable, made my early days of professional manhood (whatever that means) easier. I could be a dad, husband, DJ, coach, and businessman all in one with her by my side. But, there was nothing I hated more about her than the fact that she kept calling me 'sir'.

"Austin's fine, Deej," I pleaded, "Austin's always fine. Let's-"

She interrupted, "sir, that landing. Wow. I was standing there like, 'Ok!' You did that."

"Well, than-"

She interrupted (again), "I know Ms. Deja loved it."

My wife responded, "yes, I did very much," as she reached out for me with a smile.

Deja knew how overwhelming I found DJ to be at times. Sweet girl, just always on caffeine overload, you know? Speaking of which, she handed me the biggest cup of Ozone, dark with 5 sugars. Just how I like it. All of sudden she wasn't so annoying and pushy. It's the cycle of our relationship, even to this day. Sweet girl.

The hot coffee spilled onto my hand. I used part of my jacket to wipe the cup. I would have licked it if nobody else was there but sometimes you have to be civil. Or, at least pretend to be. There are very few extremes I won't go to for coffee. As I was wiping, Duke texted me, asking me to come across the field and make some announcements to the people. Some were loyal listeners of ours who embraced us from the very beginning. They definitely needed to hear from me.

Duke has always been a hub of good ideas. Not just the ones to get the job done, either, his ideas have always been perfect. He was situated on a platform above the field, a stone's throw away from the big campfire. Most people were congregating near the fire sipping coffee and cider, sharing small talk about the new year ahead. At least, that's what I imagined. It wasn't like I was listening to every tango of the tongue.

They buried me in 'congratulations' as I made my way to the stage. Duke finished up his famous New Jack Swing set (seriously, it's filthy how talented of a DJ he is) before handing me the microphone. I gave some speech about how grateful I was for the moment and how important family is. Even before that blue parachute. You know I'm passionate about that f-word. What better time to accentuate my campaign than then? Jake came on stage as I finished up, handing me the blue parachute before we posed for pictures under the stars of Echodale. I wonder what they were saying, those stars, watching all that emotion unfold. We were just kids ourselves, man. What were we doing? Our love just kept passing through the needles and clearing all the hurdles. It was pretty cool standing there taking photos, thinking about all of that. I felt proud. That's a good way to describe it.

***

Echodale is run by the Colesco family. They've operated mills and factories along Lake Erie since the late 1800s and never wavered. The estranged son, Mark, is the one that no one talks about. Those old Colesco Brands holiday commercials you see with the big family photos? The ones where the kids are smiling as if they're being held at gunpoint? Mark never got the invite. I almost did a story on it but he insisted that I didn't. I took a liking to him while living there. He's a man of the shadows like myself and you learn to cherish people like that before long. While his family was playing politics, he spent his time operating his sports bar on the Lux Field grounds; StarStrike. It was a neon-lit, 4 floor restaurant with the best black spiced chicken wings you'll ever have. If you ever get to Echodale, give it a try. He also had the entire joint stocked with arcade games from every decade. The perfect place to get lost. Ironically, that's where you could find me and Duke, most times.

***

Rockstars never stay to see the lights come on. We left the field once Duke's closing DJ arrived and everyone was in such a good mood. Even the people who just came to witness the moment; it was a great vibe to walk out to. We met up at StarStrike and packed out the top floor. It was always more of the party floor but really, nothing was special about it. Maybe the exclusivity was in the fact that nobody really wanted to climb 4 floors.

"So, how's radio?" asked Mark, "you guys are bringing back some good memories up there."

We smiled at each other while grabbing our wings off of the tray.

"It's radio, bro," Duke said.

Our table was full and nestled into the corner of the room like teenagers after school. Deja was sitting on my lap with our son.

"Put it like this," Duke continued while passing Essence her plate, "I love it but it's different. Like, we do it for the people, you know? So that's cool. But it's just different now."

"-yeah, I know what you mean," Mark replied, placing his tray under his arm.

Essence did that talking-with-food-in-her-mouth thing again, "well, I don't. Can you share with the class?"

"Essy," Deja chuckled.

She responded, "what? I'm just saying-" All of sudden we were sharing wings, fries, and a nervous giggle.

After calculating, Duke responded, "Ok, bet. You know how Food Boy just let all those cashiers go, right?"

"Yeah-" He continued, "now you get to the register and it's all self-checkout. Just that one old lady watching everybody?"

Duke loved to talk with his hands. Like a baptist preacher. The table was glued to him and he was just getting started. Intellectually magnetizing, always has been. Essence had taken too big of a bite and couldn't talk, but she nodded. It was more like a *go on* type of nod as opposed to agreement.

Duke obliged, "that's it. That's the tweet."

Poor Essence. I thought she was going to hurt herself trying to make sense of it all. Sometimes I wonder how she got through all those years at City Hall.

"Ah, the digital age," Mark affirmed.

Another voice at the table asked, "so, it's just a bunch of computers?"

Duke's smug was coming alive.

He replied, "that Food Boy example? Exactly that. We're just some of the lucky few. Well, blessed."

Mark replied, "the world is changing, man. Actually, I'll say it's changed. Things are certainly different."

"They are," said Duke, "and watch this. How often do you listen to the radio now?"

Mark bobbed his head, "well, I still listen often. Especially to Rumble."

"Yeah, you're an old school type of guy. You don't count. No offense but not you," Duke laughed, "what about y'all? You listen?"

Essence (who finally finished that one wing) replied, "I mean, yeah, when-"

"No, you don't," Duke interjected, "whenever I'm in the car with you, you got something else on. Don't even try it."

Essence pleaded, "No, I was 'gonna say that I listen when I don't have anything else to listen to. Whenever I do, though, y'all sound good."

"Well thank you," Duke said with a smile. "But, yeah."

I decided that Duke had fought enough and it was time for a sentence, or two, from me.

"Yeah, it's about opportunity. We're up against the wall right now. Industry's squeezed," I said to Mark.

He was always engaged by these types of conversations although I don't think he was ever being nosy, or anything. It always came from a place of genuine concern for both us and business. A loving pry.

He asked, "-you talked to any of your teammates lately?"

I wouldn't have taken that bite if I knew he was going to ask me another question.

"Yeah, all the time," I hastened the chew, "Armonti's actually coming to Toronto next weekend."

"Aye," Duke interjected, "that boy has been wild this year."

I nodded, "naw, he really has."

This is when Deja dropped her little fingers into my basket of fries. *Did I say 'my'? I meant 'our'.* It always felt like we were Mark's favorite because the fries, wings, and everything else he brought out was always perfect. Like, the right temperature and everything. Sharing is certainly caring except when eating at StarStrike. Then it's kind of every man (and woman) for themselves. Ah, I love my wife.

"Biggest contract in the league, he better be playing like it. 'Gotta start hitting those free throws, though."

Derry had been rather quiet but the sounds of basketball talk woke him.

"Ah, lefthand. Those shots are never free." He wasn't eating, "I wish they'd stop calling it that. Messes up the game."

The Loganberry tea steamed in front of him. You guessed it, his legs were crossed and his face was decorated with joy. I was just happy to hear his voice each time he talked. Our final days in Paradise really made me question if we'd see each other again.

"Well, I don't know if I can go that far," Duke replied. Derry sipped the tea.

"Oh, but I can. In fact I did," Derry rose up in his seat, leaning over the table. "You see, my boy. What if it wasn't free? What if you had to earn it?"

"I just think you're going too deep, bro," Duke said with a smirk. "Bottom line is, Armonti and them can't win it all until he hits them shots."

"They got to get some help under the cup, too," I interjected.

This was right before that big trade fiasco. It turned the league upside down.

Deja chimed in from my lap, "well, they still got to beat L.A and we all know that ain't happening."

"See? That's why I love you," Duke joined. We giggled like a family sitcom. "-That right there is why you're the goat," Duke pointed at Deja.

I looked toward the bathroom area. It was in a weird place on the top floor, off in the corner behind the Time Crisis games. There was a brief narrow hallway that sucked you into the bathroom area, dark and desolate. She was standing there. That red lotus. I had wondered where she had drifted off to after we landed. I wish you could have seen those eyes, tantalizing and gentle, dancing on her brown skin. Her fingers had these long nails and she used the left pointer to invite me into the dark corner.

"Austin, honey," Deja said into my daze, "you good?"

"I'm fine. Just have to use the bathroom. Be right back."

***

The next few moments would have been a great introduction to a horror film. It felt slow and dramatic. I was lulled by the sounds of all the arcade games as I began walking into the dark corner. There was music playing but I could only hear the bass. Well, feel it, rather. The room tilted and the neon lights were all pointing towards her. She continued to wag that slender finger.

"Come," she whispered.

It echoed over everything else. Just drowned it right out. Except for the bass from the music, I could always feel that.

Fourscore winters later (hehe), I arrived at the corridor and she led me to the bathroom door. We were holding hands. Get this, she opens the door and throws me up against the tile. Well, I should say pushed me because my back was against the wall. The red lotus gets close and holds her face just a few inches away from mine. She's staring up at me and I'm staring down at her, my eyes wide as chopped zucchini.

"You shouldn't be here," I pleaded.

Maybe I sounded a little too nervous. At that point of my life, she seemed to respond better to my calm tone. Details matter in those honeymoon phases.

"Listen, now is not the time," I took a deep breath, "later."

Her smile turned sadistic and strangled me. The corners of her golden lips wrapped knots around my throat and the walls started shrinking. It was weird and painful as hell. Then, the bathroom door swung open. The wind screamed in the highest of keys.

"Big bro!" a voice said from the threshold.

It was Devin. He was dressed in his service uniform and extended his arms for a hug. He made it. Missed the skydive, but made it.

"Congratulations, man," he said as he stared into my eyes.

The sweat gave me away. My forehead felt like I got caught in a monsoon. Without an umbrella, duh. I fell into his arms and hugged him tight. My eyes were still searching for the lotus but my heart was just fine in my brother's arms. I was happy to see that man.

3 VETERANS IN THE BATHROOM II

"Another episode?" Devin asked.

He pulled out a navy blue handkerchief and wiped my face. I was paralyzed by the muffled crowd and arcade sounds buzzing outside of the bathroom door. I had just snapped back into reality. I looked around for the lotus but she slipped away like water down a drain.

"Yeah?" he asked again.

"You know it."

"Yeah, man I'm right there with you," he said, walking to the sink, "but you know what, bro? We keep on going."

"Yeah we do."

"You'breathing straight?" he asked.

"Yeah, nah I'm good. It wasn't bad or anything. You know I just get into my head sometimes."

"What'd she have on this time?" he asked.

He took the last paper towel from the dispenser, wet it, and handed it to me. I held it on my forehead. It was one of those unwritten remedies in our family. That, or ginger ale. That stuff will save the world someday.

"Wait a minute, who's the big brother here? You askin' all the questions," I finally responded.

You should have seen the face I was making. He chuckled and we shared a moment. We felt the memories of growing up together, playing in the basement, trying to hide the trouble we were causing. We weren't bad kids but we were like evil angels. Like, we always meant well but sometimes we just made a big mess. Then we'd giggle about it because it was our thing. The trouble was our little secret. Well, the full story was our secret, I should say.

***

The toilet flushed and dipshit waddled out of the stall. He rocked on his bow legs and was adjusting the buckles on his kelly green dive suit. Devin and myself were still giggling but I could hear that we both were surprised by dipshit. It would have been nice to introduce the two but what do I say? *Devin, I'd like you to meet dipshit?* Then I remembered that his name was actually Jebbs.

"You fellas 'right?" Jebbs asked, walking to the sink.

They stared at each other's stripes. It was something about those American flags that did it for them. I never felt that but I guess that's what the service does to you. Personally, I've always struggled to see past America's scars. Maybe we'll talk about politics later.

"Oh, Jebbs. Didn't even know you were in here. This is my brother, Devin," I extended to my new friend, "bro, this is Jebbs. One of the guys from the dive."

"Sir, it's an honor. Thank you for your service," my brother said humbly.

Man, I was so proud watching him stand there with his chest out. He had grown into a fine young man.

Jebbs grinned, "well, yeah! Also to you, young man."

They shook hands. The scene was odd, but I was just happy to have my brother in town.

Jebbs asked Devin (felt like I was ignored from this point on), "things good with y'all?" Devin affirmed so and Jebbs looked to me, "the more you sweat in peace, the less you bleed in war."

Oh, dipshit.

My brother looked at me with his eyebrows dancing on the ceiling. Mine jumped back at him. Jebbs was a master of something, for sure. Don't know what it was but it was something. There's another word I would use to describe him but I promised you I wouldn't use it anymore.

***

We were silent leaving the bathroom. After all of those pleasantries, inhaling urine together, only our footsteps were talking on the way out. Jebbs must have had somewhere to go because he cut straight for the elevator.

***

"Now I can hug you like I want to," Devin said to my bride.

"Mmmmmmm," Deja replied with miles and miles of love.

Heart bubbles floated around them like an anime scene. The only person not paying attention was Duke. Some mild wings had his heart. Fries too.

Derry climbed out of his seat, "Devin, my boy," he said, "l'eroe!"

If you thought he towered over Deja you should have seen Devin standing next to Derry. The two men shook hands before Devin went back into the sky. He went around the table and greeted everyone before Duke pulled him into a conversation.

"Bro, let me ask you. You're single, right?"

Devin replied, "uh oh."

"Nah. Nah. Just follow me, I won't pull you into any trouble," Duke chewed, "you single right?"

My little brother was overwhelmed. He had this look he made whenever the moment escaped him. Surprised and frozen. If you cooked it any longer, it could've been taken as disrespect. He always meant well though.

Finally he responded, "...kinda."

"Ok, he said 'kinda'. Nevermind then, bro."

"Nah, go ahead and ask him. Don't get shy, now," Essence pleaded.

"You right. His girl not here," Duke began (now I'm getting nervous for Devin), "would you have a threesome with two people you just met? Like in a club, or something? If you were single, of course."

"Like, in the club?" my brother tip-toed.

"I mean, like, you all met at the club," Duke responded, "because somebody here said they would. I'm not 'gon say no names."

Essence replied, "na uh, don't do that. That is not what I said. Don't believe this man. I-"

That's when I tuned out. Essence and Duke always went back and forth like that. It'll drive you insane if you listen to too much of it. You'll feel your IQ slip away by the sentence, their verbal tennis was exhausting. It was always love though. They really were great friends deep down inside. Both of them just had an affinity for soapboxes. You know what I had an affinity for? Deja's eyes. Honestly, that's what saved me from Duke and Essence's rambling.

I turned my head away from them briefly and looked down at my empty plate. When I looked back down the table, Deja's eyes were blocking my view. They were singing all sorts of sweet songs. Stevie Wonder, Anita Baker, Marvin Gaye; they were all there. Those pupils were glowing loud enough for me to hear all of the joys from our past, future, and even our present. We were going to be parents for the first time. Our eyes said that to each other. I guess you can say our smiles were doing a little talking too. Much louder than that noise at the end of the table. Derry was watching us watch each other and his eyes joined in. He was proud and polished, his collar began to glow. Then I found Deja's eyes again and this time they were singing a much different tune. In fact, they weren't singing at all. Those eyes were telling me it was time to go so I went and found Mark for the checks.

Let's cut to the chase here, my card was declined. Yes, it got awkward and silent while I was pretending to not understand how that could happen. Difficult times. I mean, the air just left the arcade without any concern for life. I felt like everyone was looking at me with shame but then I realized that the "everyone" looking at me was only me. All of the voices laughing at the *broke black man* were my voices. There wasn't anyone around. It was just me and Mark standing at the cashier's desk in the corner of the room. He was such a good friend.

"We've been having issues with these all day. Don't worry about it, we'll take care of you and Deja's," he said to me.

Don't think for a second they were really having issues with their equipment. Everyone else's payments went through just fine. I knew that the basketball money had run dry and I had no more mirages to wish upon. And to think, I'm about to be someone's father.

4 BROWN WINGTIPS

Duke walked up and rested his arm on my shoulder. I was surrounded by love, the deep and hearty kind. He didn't know anything about the payment but he did know that each meal was quite the hunt. After all, we do work for the same people in the same industry. That desert was big enough for the two of us; it just didn't have any more resources. Ample space to build mirages but only puddles of water. You know? Nothing sustainable.

> "See you tomorrow? 'Gonna head out," Duke said while patting my shoulder, "let's light it up tomorrow."

I nodded and affirmed before heading out myself. The ride home was silent. There wasn't any of that tension that haunts some couples in the car. I think the silence was more of a response to the hurricane of thoughts we each were experiencing. Like, in our separate lives and at home.

The passenger seat was cold. Deja had both hands on the wheel (yup, she's one of those types). I put my hand on her thigh. I just wanted to touch her. We glanced at each other with that quirky early-romance smile. You know the one that makes older, more tenured couples sick. She turned back to focus on the road and turned up the volume on that woman they called "The Donna". She ended up hosting late-night TV before dying in that skiing accident (swear she didn't even get to finish her first week on the air). Deja was a lifestyle enthusiast and she couldn't get enough of that lady. Whatever "The Donna" said was gospel to her. If we're being honest, that's the reason why she finally went hybrid. "The Donna" published a feature that claimed 'hybrid-moms' live longer, and well, now we charge her car for a few hours before we hit the road. I guess it's just me polluting the world with my V-8, supercharged chariot. Maybe I'll convert one day.

***

Our parking lot was always beautiful in the winter. Echodale loved snow even if they hated it. You can only fight something for a few rounds before it's just best to embrace it. Then, that's when things get better.

I've told you about our apartment before and it was as cozy as you could remember. There weren't too many words between us as we settled in that night. We kind of just jumped right into bed. She nestled under my arms with her hands wrapped around her belly. My left hand joined hers and we held our baby boy. She went to sleep and I was scrolling on my phone. It was an interesting contrast reading the headlines. Made me question if I really wanted to bring a kid into this mess. Our world was a small party with 10 DJs playing at the same time. Good luck trying to find the rhythm. But I knew that I had no choice but to lead this dance and that's what I thought about as I turned the light out that night.

***

The snow built up overnight but we made it to work. I still remember my opener til this day, '*Rumble 93, shaking up Echodale, I'm Austin Arringon*' and whatever else I had to say at that moment. I was in that weird point of my career where people were still fresh on what happened in Paradise. Some had forgotten me as a basketball star but never forgot me as Gerard's best friend. Then some people of Echodale didn't care about any of that and just fell in love with hearing me on the radio. I was really beginning to sound good. After all, that is what my undergraduate degree was in.

It was weird laughing on the radio while dodging texts from bill collectors. Sometimes we'd be talking on air and my phone would just be buzzing in the background. I'd take a look at it and just drop my head. Duke knew that look, too. We were tired but we always gave the people our best. That's just how we're built. You knew that from my days at State; we didn't get those championships because I was weak-hearted. But like I said, we were tired.

"-say, Duke," I said through the glass (and over the air) as he was mixing, "last night was a great night, wasn't it? Fell from the sky with the Air Force, shout out to Fort Dennings. Found out me and the lady are having a boy."

Duke chimed in with his DJ voice, "that's facts. Congratulations, by the way, bro."

"Well, thank you sir. Went and had a great night at StarStrike, shout out to Mark Colesco."

Duke did it again, "the homie."

"Oh, and my baby brother, Devin pulled up! He was late and missed the dive but he is in town. Shout out to Devin." My tone slowed down over the lulling instrumental in the background, "we've had great times at Rumble but today's it. There's so much going on right now, family, it's time."

THE OTHER BLUE

Duke smiled at me through the glass. The glare was trying to block our eye contact but all I had to do was shift forward a little bit. I think he was happy at how I delivered that message, it was almost as smooth as that landing that I said I wouldn't talk about again.

I carried on about all the people I would miss working with and the memories we've made with the Echodale community but I stopped short of getting choked up. Only happy emotions, that's all I wanted to share with the people. I made sure everyone knew that we weren't leaving the Echodale community and that we'd still be very active. It was true.

Deja knew this was going to happen and she was very supportive; not just of me but of my peace. It was a hard conversation to have but things are hard sometimes, you know that. It happened just before the holidays. Here's how it went:

***

"Mrs. Dortch's cat got out again," Deja marched into the apartment. "She was on the steps. I could have tripped and dropped the bags, damnz."
"Austin?" she questioned over the TV.

I think I was watching Seattle and Miami.

"Hold on, mom (she and her mom talked every night after work, no matter how late she got in). Let's see where he is, I'll call you back."

"You tell my boy I said 'ello. Don't be over there kickin' people's cat, baby," her mother said.

I used to love her voice. You could taste the Carolina pride in it; sweet, spicy, and loving. She was fairly young for her age.

> I reached for the ceiling while laying on the couch, "hi mom! I'm over here. Watching the game."

> "Oh, you over there. I thought you were in the bedroom or something," Deja walked into the room, "that Dortch lady really doesn't care about her cats."

I didn't either.

> "Jojo got let go today," I smacked.

> Deja replied, "no way. Joanne? She's been there forever."

> "I know."

> She continued, "and she's so sweet. Remember she gave us those wine glasses? That's sad." The mother (to be) came over her. She knelt in front of me, "We should talk about it."

I stared at her for a few seconds before rising up on the couch.

> "She was about to go on air. Like, it was probably like, 9:58, or something. Yeah… Because the morning show was out of the studio, so it definitely was later, around then.They didn't even let her do her first report- "

"Terrible. Came to work and everything," Deja said.

"Exactly. I just don't get it. She's so quiet and out'the way. Then they walked her out like she was a criminal, or something."

"No they did not, nu'uh," Deja said. I nodded but more so with my eyebrows than my head. I don't know if that makes sense but that's what I did.

"And still haven't explained anything to me. We just skipped the news like nothing happened. You know Duke's been blowing me up."

She put those soft hands on my hardened skin. No massage, just her touch.

"Ok, for real," her eyes spoke into mine, "are you worried that you'll be out too?"

"After Paradise? Hell no. I mean, can't put anything past those assholes but they'd be foolish to do that. I think it's just more so unsettling to be around. It's not even scary, it's just annoying. The people deserve better."

"We do. Because honestly? I loved JoJo. I know Bell did, too. Like, she is really good at her job," Deja said.

"That's how I know she'll be fine. She'll probably end up working with y'all or 'The Z'. But, still."

Deja shook her head, "did she announce anything, yet?"

"Not on her page. I don't blame her, for real. That's tough."

It got silent. Well, except for the cat scratching the door. We could almost hear the snow falling as we were staring at each other, her hand on top of mine. My heart had been bulging out of my chest all day, like my lungs were playing doubledutch. All of that settled. Her heart came out too. It was doing pirouettes with beautiful pink ribbons trailing its every move. It lured my inner thoughts out of their shell.

"I've got to get Impact going."

"Yes! You do. Just set the goal and get out. You already know where I'm at over here," she said with a challenging look on her face, "show up and shut it down. Every time. I believe in this right here."

She rested her finger on my sternum. This is around the time she fell in love with fingernail art and I could tell that she just got hers done. It kind of tickled. It felt comforting to be believed in, though. That's love, too.

***

That night, we laid in bed for hours. It was somber at first because of my mood but before long, we started giggling like schoolyard kids. We loved to leave the blinds open during snow storms because it was exciting watching the flakes fall. Just two kids from the east coast enjoying

Mother Nature's cold tantrum. When I retired and shared that story with my psychiatrist, Dr. Eklovonian, she believed that our love of snow was our way of staying connected to home. It served as an anchor of nostalgia, if you will. A neverending beacon pointing us to love.

When the conversation slowed and we finally became tired, I told Deja that I planned on leaving the station after the gender reveal. I had some money saved up and my 216 page business plan for Impact was just about complete. At 216 pages, I'm sure it was past complete. Looking back on that now I can't help but smile because our company became successful once we simplified all of that. That's usually how things work though. 'Gotta do it the hard way first.

The plan was simple:

> 1) Jump out of the plane
> 2) Quit the station
> 3) Take a week to myself
> 4) Launch Impact.

But you should know by now that my life rarely goes according to plan. Let's go back to step 2.

***

"Well, that was fun," I said sarcastically to Duke through the glass. He was breaking down his DJ equipment.

"It's done, now," he laughed, "just be ready for sha-"

The studio door barged open.

"You guys are done?" screamed our old boss, Chester Shaden. What a guy. "No. You've got to be shittin' me, Austin."

"It's time, Shade."

He walked over to the console, "hey, Duke. Unpack, buddy. Just stay a little longer and you guys party. T-Tell... Tell everyone this isn't true. You guys were joking, right? What'd ya say?"

Poor Shade. It wasn't that he loved us that much, he just felt powerless. Don't be fooled. That's how this game worked. It was one big power struggle with guys measuring dicks all day. It never was my thing and that's why we had to leave. We had to make room for what really was my calling. One of the best days of my life, in retrospect.

He looked at me, "Austin, what'd ya say? Stay? You guys are doing great, man. The building's already just about empty. I need you. What'd ya say?"

If his eyes could talk, they wouldn't. They were drowned in sorrow.

"It's time, Shade."

The door swung open, again. It was the midday girl, DebbsOne. She was a sweet and petite DJ from Echodale with a golden smile. Very humble young woman. Went on to do some good work across the border but I haven't talked to her in a while. I'll never forget her face that day though. She walked in as if the floor was made of thin glass with a sea of piranha's swimming beneath who hadn't eaten since the cold war. Frantic little thing, that lady. She was walking in the studio but her soul was still in the car.

"No, no, no, no," Shaden marched to the studio door, "not right now, Debs. Give us a minute. Just- a minute, or two."

"Name your price, kid," He leaned up against the door (with sweet little Debbs on the other side), I thought he was going to have a heart attack. "You got it. Any- anything you guys need."

"It's not about money. It's just time. You'll find someone else. You know how this business works."

He dropped his head. It didn't matter how long of a beat he took to find words. There was nothing he could say, nor was there a check that he could write to keep me and Duke on the air. We made up our minds and had already begun living our lives beyond radio.

"Hello! Rumble 93!" I began answering the phones.

They were blinking like stop lights in the middle of the night. Every single line was busy and buzzing. We expected that, though. We really put on a good show but more than anything, we were honest. That honest radio (or media, for that matter) is undefeated. Shade stood there chasing his breath as I answered those calls. He heard all of those people wish us well and say how they wouldn't support the station anymore. Or, how much they were going to miss hearing us in the morning. I didn't do it on purpose, it's just customary to clear the phone lines before the next jock comes in. Old school radio etiquette but good practice, nonetheless.

"Yo! Rumble 93!"

Muttering

"Hello?"

You have a prepaid call. You will not be charged for this call. This call is from the New York State Penitentiary, inmate number 5-9-4-3-8-A-5-A.

"Hello?"

"...Austin's leaving us, huh," a scratchy voice said.

He sounded like he was straining on the toilet. That kind of straining of the voice, you know? Except it was his natural voice. I could tell.

"Yes sir, this is it for us. We appreciate your support, though."

"But you don't even know who you're talking to, buddy."

"Ok," I laughed a bit, *"well, who's this?"*

"Dale Mangold."

My heart fell down my throat, into my intestinal tract, banging the walls all the way down. I felt the rush of a bowel movement. My heart started kicking my bladder, too. My fingertips were throbbing and my tongue was hiding behind my teeth. My body started to tremble as if we were buried under upstate snow. Confidence escaped my eyes like a slave in the night, after master suffered a surprise heart attack. I swear I saw the lights flicker.

5 PLAYING ON MY PHONE

Goddamn Dale Mangold.

"Hey, Dale," Shade begged while walking over to the phone, "he's leaving me. Can you believe this shit? Tell him to stay, would'cha?"

Desperation is always a turn off. Not that he had a sliver of hope, but even if there was, Shade's desperation would have choked it. He was leaning over the console on the edges of his brown wing-tipped shoes. He always wore those. Either the brown ones or the black ones. I could sense that he was being rather lighthearted with his tone but he had no clue who Mangold was. He should have because I told him the story a million times. Maybe it just didn't register to him.

"Well, say something," Shade said to me.

Pushy little man. I really was frozen though. The only iceberg in the melted tundra, floating away on a pain that only I could feel. It was a weird moment. So I started looking around the room, hoping I could find some balance. That's when I noticed her; the red lotus. She was sitting in the corner of the studio with her legs crossed on the desk; beautiful, brown legs. You remember those 'Jasper Says' dolls that came out a few years ago? The ones that freaked everybody out? She had one of those in her lap and she was caressing it, gently, and was brushing its hair. Then, her song. It was that same tune from the plane the night before. She was humming it. Then, she cut me with her smile. It was scary, but comforting.

"Dale, you can't be here."

Shade lept back so fast, his thick glasses tried to run away, "wai- wait, -wait. Kid."

I hung up the call.

"Jesus, Austin. What the hell was that? You're trying to make things worse for us, now? Come on, Pal," Shade wagged his finger. "Come o-"

"Shade, you're full of shit. You know that?"

"Yeah, yeah. You'll be replaced tomorrow. Y'always can be replaced," he continued out the door, "clear my studio, would'ya? Please don't make me call anyone."

***

The term 'emotional roller coaster' really pisses me off. I love roller coasters, so it never translated well for me. I'll just say that moment was like an 'emotional and illegal roller coaster'. One that doesn't have fun drops and whipping speeds. No cameras to pose for so you can brag about how brave you are. This (illegal, or whatever I called it) emotional roller coaster was a death wish. I had braced myself for quitting my job but I had no clue **that** asshole was 'gonna call in. I also didn't know that Shade was going to spend 20 minutes seesawing my heartstrings about leaving, only to get upset and storm out. The red lotus slammed her doll on the counter and walked over to unplug my headphones. She grabbed my jacket and dawned my broad shoulders without saying a word. Faint music was playing over the air. The TV was on mute but it was making that weird sound of it being on. That high pitched buzzing sound that actually is more of a feeling than something audible. I wasn't calm but she was calm for me. The red lotus led me to my car and I waved at Debbs, staring through her frozen windshield. I don't know what was wider, her eyes or her rims.

***

I didn't say much for the next few hours. My car was silent which is unusual for me because I love to listen to sports radio or a network news broadcast. You know what was loud, though? My stomach.

I ended up at one of my favorite places to grab a hoagie in Echodale; the Upside Down Plaza. It was downtown, a few blocks away from the train station. Its claim to fame was a 7 floor parking garage sitting on top of an underground 3-floor food pavilion. Upside down. It had a restaurant named Waysmith's. I doubt it's still there today, but the hoagies were something serious. I'd go there twice a week and sit in the back corner of their dining room, planning out my shows for the next few days (as best as I could, at least). They had this huge tilescreen and they'd play sports highlights on it whenever I walked in. Now that I think about it, the hoagies were great, but it was about more than the food. Those trips to Waysmith's were more about peace than steak. I needed both after that exhausting (last) day at Rumble.

Sheila threw down her apron and greeted me at the door, "Austin! Happy Friday, hon."

"Happy Friday, Sheila. Even though it feels like yesterday was Friday."

"Well, you're always doing something somewhere, gosh. I bet. Time just runs away, huh?" she said as she led me to my corner. "It's been moving slow around here." "Coffee?"

"Tea."

Sheila bit, "tea? Uh oh. 'Guess it isn't too much of a happy Friday, huh?"

"You know? It's going."

"Lemon on the side?" she said walking away.

"That's cool. Thank you."

It wasn't the job, it was Dale. I hadn't spoken to him since, well, I don't think I've ever actually spoken to him, honestly. I only remember being a few feet away from him during his arraignment, trying not to jump over the bench and strangle that shitbag.

"Well if it isn't the *Padre'* to be," Big June walked over to the table. He was the owner. He died of a heart attack on the kitchen floor a few years after that day. "Congratulations, my son."

His stomach sat down before he did, but they both were welcome. He was just the voice that I needed to hear that day. He'd been through so much opening Waysmith's. Even more trying to keep it open. The Rush (football team) brought him here to play Right Guard but injuries cut his career short. That's why you never heard of him. He had a great career at Syracuse, though. Think he's a record holder of some sort. Name on the wall and everything. Plus, he was a father. Sheila is his youngest of 7.

"You're drinking tea today. That's far from champagne," he fished.

"Well, you guys don't have champagne, remember?"

"Ah-hah." He always did this pointing thing with his eyes. "I meant **your** champagne. That caffeine."

My smile waned and a breeze settled.

"I quit my job today."

"Good. Fuck 'em," he huffed and puffed. "Somedays I see you drag in here and I think 'man, that kid is a star. What's he doing fooling with Shade and Co? That guys a tool. You deserve better. So…Fuck'em. Better days, kid."

He could see that I swallowed his words but I was having a tough time digesting them.

"Listen, it's a boy right?"

"Huh?"

58

"The kid! Your kid. A boy right?"

"Oh, yeah. Scary as -"

"No, no, no. Listen. Everything is going to be a'ight. You've got some time before Deja delivers, time to, you know- figure things out. Tie up the loose ends. It's hard for you because you're a good man and you just want it all to be right.... and it will. But you know what that kid will really appreciate? Having a father who has the nuts to make the tough decisions when it's time. It'ain't easy and it'aint for everybody."

"Thanks, June."

"You're welcome. Whatever you need, you're welcome. When I was living under that fucking bridge, rats as big as dogs, I said I'd never go back. I'd never go back to living by other people's rules and waiting for someone to call the play. Fuck'em. Waysmith's wouldn't be a thing if I still thought like that. Fuck'em. You hear me?"

Loud and clear. His voice echoed into the rest of my life. You see I'm still talking about it today. We related on the sports thing. We were raised on someone calling plays, making plans, and us just going through the motions for the team. It became second nature. What do you expect though? I was 5 years old the first time I picked up a basketball. We only had 3 plays in little league, but that's where it all began. That's when I started staring at the sidelines before making a decision.

The alarm on my phone blared. I knew that time had slipped away from me but I didn't feel bad about it because, well, what a day? Right?

"Hey, can we change this? Deja's on," I said to Big June. He smiled like a proud father.

"Oh, yes. Of course," he said, "Tony! Hit the switch!"

Tony yelled, "what!"

"The switch! Hit the switch!" There were 5 other customers in there and they all were looking at our table now. You should have seen their faces. "Jesus, Tony. What're 'ya good for, eh?" Big June marched over to the counter.

"I always seem to treat your mother right," Tony barked back.

"Hey (he dragged this word out for miles)," Big June stared at Tony. "Austin, she's on 2, right?"

"Yes sir!" I hollered into their side of the shop.

Those two kept bickering like teenage step brothers. The sports highlights ended and the real show came on. There she was. My 4 o'clock dose of joy condensed into my dream of a wife. I was so proud of her. Still am. She was still climbing the ranks in Echodale but she swallowed every ounce of screentime. It was like she was made for it, you know? The rest of life would show and prove that theory. Those early days were some of my favorites, though. She would come on right after 4 with her report for the day. It was never long (at that time) but it was always just right. The people of Echodale trusted her and she delivered. Even while she was waiting to deliver herself.

I'm Donna French.

And, I'm Ken Prescott, welcome to 2 at 4. Before we get to what's happening in Echodale, we want to take the time to say congratulations to our very own, Deja Arrington.

That's right, Ken. She's a lovely young lady, isn't she?

Yes, she is. One of our favorites here at Channel 2. And she's having a boy. Congratulations to her and her husband, Austin Arrington.

Skydiving gender reveal.

Yes, quite the scene there. Look at that blue parachute. That was at Lux Field last night.

What a moment. Alright, congratulations Deja and Austin.

[shuffling papers]

"Congratulations, honey," Sheila snuck into my right peripheral.

More importantly, she had my hoagie dressed nicely, hanging off the plate like a retired slob.

-holiday spirit here in Echodale at the Dexter plant for their third annual Kevin Dexter toy drive.

The city and Dexter CEO, Jon Dexter, say that this year's drive will bring holiday cheer to over 1 million kids in Echodale.

Our Deja Arrington is out at the Dexter plant with more, Deja.

"I… Well-"

Poor Deja. She's always been a mega-professional (and a borderline crazed perfectionist) when it came to her work. That's what helped her climb the ladder so fast. She was always about her business. But, she just couldn't keep it together at the Dexter plant.

We talked about it later that night with our legs curled together in front of the TV. Yes, of course the cat was outside of our front door, scratching away. It always wanted to be saved.

Deja told me that she had no clue her anchors would congratulate us like that. When I jumped out of that plane (still can't believe I did something so foolish), neither of us knew that the news cameras were there. It was almost like they wanted to conceal it themselves. It made sense though because everyone at Channel 2 was sweet. They really were a special part of our lives. Not just then, but forever.

***

THE OTHER BLUE

We fell asleep on the couch that night and the next few days were a bit difficult. It was the very beginning of my learning how to manage freedom. I didn't have a single client but I spent some time working on advertising and branding. That's when I decided to make Impact's colors red and black. It just worked. The red was bold and commanding, plus it reminded me of my days at State. The black was as powerful as the color of my skin and the centuries of strength behind it.

Those days were quiet except for the banking app notifications scaring me half to hell. I hadn't made a dime but that didn't mean the expenses would wait (though, that would be nice, wouldn't it?). Early days of small business are tough. I was wearing these black reading glasses a lot, too. Wasn't a lick of medicine in them. A lot of the business guys I'd met over the years were wearing them so I did the same. That was a weird period of me trying to find myself all over again. It had happened so much that I worried it would continue for the rest of my life. As I got older, I started to appreciate the reinvention process and fell in love with getting better. It takes maturity to see the world through that lens. Try it, if you haven't already.

***

I was never alone. The red lotus would spend those days walking around the room, helping me organize notes for the website, or the business plan (which everyone mentions but never asks for). She's gorgeous, I swear. Some days it was the red dress and other days it was this red sweatsuit covered with a puffy red vest. I was the optimist and she was my partner from hell. Not a drop of negativity went unclaimed by her. It wasn't like she was bringing it to the business, or anything like that. She was more like amoxicillin. It'll have you shitting and throwing up all over the place but it also finds the infection. Gets it right out of you. It's a dirty job but someone has to do it. Unless you want to be infected. Then, no one has to do it.

One day, my phone rang and it was the hospital. Surely you've heard about Echodale's massive medical campuses. *No?* That's part of what made it the city it is today, that medical stuff. This call was from Galloway General (Central Campus), the biggest of the 6 hospitals. I had been asked to come down and ID a body. Deja was at work already so it was just me and the red lotus.

6 LIFE'S WEIRD

I know suspense is what sells the story but don't panic. My immediate family was nowhere near Echodale. Me and Deja were transplants, remember? That's not to say that Duke, Essence, Derry, or others in town didn't matter. I just didn't want you thinking the absolute worst. That sounds bad, I know. It's all I was thinking about after I finally decided to head down to the hospital. Thankfully, Devin called and I had someone else to share this with.

He mumbled, "a body?"

"Right. Wh-"

He interjected, "bro. **A body?** You-uh, you checked the number, right? Like-"

"Came up clean when they called, bro. It was this hospital downtown, Galloway General. It was green."

He continued, "that's fucking wild. Like, you heard from those people at the table that night, right?"

"At StarStrike? Was it an arcade type of place?"

"Yeah," he shot.

"I mean, I haven't heard from Mark since that night, for real. But... If something happened to him I would have heard about it by now. Ev-everybody else… Derry text me. I still have to respond, actually. I know Essence is working in Toronto this weekend -"

"- that's my boo," I heard him smile.

"Yeah, she is pretty," I laughed, "but she's not your speed, bro."

"I know. But she fine, though," he laughed back, "that's wild though, bro. Like, you sure you 'wanna go?"

"I'm here now. I'll hit you later."

Whoever you're thinking about right now; the person you think I'm ID'ing, it's probably them. My life had become so extreme that I stopped trying to fight moments like these. I just admitted that my life probably will never be considered "normal". Who decides that anyway, yeah? You just have to live your life and the tracks that are set before you. Apparently, these were mine that day because no matter how confused and concerned I was, I still felt driven to go.

***

The lady at the front desk of the morgue was pale and dead herself. Her breath smelled like bathwater mildewing in an old shoe. When she talked, I didn't know if it was her speaking or the gigantic mole on her face. Not that there's anything wrong with moles because you see I have a few. It was just something about hers that I never forgot.

"Sign this," she threw papers at me.

Thankfully they didn't fly away because I would have walked out.

> She continued to a lady, "but the stiff comes'n here, nurse is going bat-shit cur-ray-zee. It's that new one, from Bah-ston. I'm like, sweetheart, you might be in the wrong jig, you know?"

> "Oh no, the blonde. I know who you're talking about," her coworker (much nicer lady, brighter too) replied.

Her eyes didn't reply at all, though. In fact, her entire face didn't hear a single word that the old lady said.

> "Honey, yes. Almost dropped the stiff," she said turning back to me, "are you done?"

I was. I had signed my name and officially declared myself to identify the body for the Echodale police. Some of the ink dripped out of that old pen onto my shirt. It was only a little, though.

> She continued her never-ending tale, "-so the mortician comes in. Minka. Big guy over at-"

> Then a deeper, much warmer voice called my attention, "Mr. Arrington."

Too bad his eyes were glued to that clipboard. I was thinking he would be nicer than the lady at the front desk but he just had a deeper, warmer voice. The deception.

"Thank you for coming," he clicked his heels down the hall. "Especially in the dark, like this. You were listed as next to kin. We tried sorting this out without you… Just the records on file- they're all dead. No pun in-"

He stopped at the end of the hall. His beady eyes found mine.

"Nevermind, that's inappropriate. Please, this way."

It was a room full of big cold drawers. I didn't touch anything but I could see how cold they were. In fact, they told me themselves. That's when I officially asked myself *what the hell am I doing here?* The one light in the room spotlighted a body in the middle, draped in a spotless sheet. It must have been the biggest one they had because it was damn near dragging on the floor. I had already begun trying to piece together this mystery, measuring the body with my eyes. Don't think that I was walking around or anything, though. I was scared shitless deep down inside.

A door closed gently behind me. Two men, middle aged and far too serious, walked in with their trench coats sweeping the floors. The one with the bald patch on top of his head must have been the leader of the two because he spoke first.

"I'm Detective Lattisaw and this is Detective Mederra. Thank you for coming," he said with a handshake. "Doc, you've got some gloves?"

"Of course I do. Here's one pair, here's one pair, and- here's another. And," he did this weird glide-move across the floor, right past the dead guy. Or, girl, for that matter. "-and here's another." I looked down as he was handing me the gloves thinking *why do I need these?*

"Now, I must say. Warn you, rather," the other detective decided to speak, "this one is a bit tough on the stomach. If'this is a loved one, I am sorry. Any information you can offer, son… We'll take it." He rested his hand on my shoulder.

"I hope I can be of help because I.. don't have…any family in Echodale. Or, anywhere near here. I guess that's why this is so di-"

"Well, still," Detective Lattisaw interrupted, "you're on this paper. Let's just see if it's anything y'can offer. If not, then so be'it. 'Just a lot of nothing here and we're trying to make it something. For the people."

Just because I understood didn't mean I cared or was fine with it. You know how poignant curiosity can be sometimes. We see some things and start certain fires that we just have to watch burn. This was that. I thought, *shit, I'm here now.* They unfolded the sheet and her breasts greeted me first. I turned my head.

"Sorry about that," the damned doctor said before rolling the sheet back up, exposing just her face. "There we go, sweetheart."

The detectives stretched their gloves loud and very dramatic. You would have thought they were about to do surgery on network television. One of those doctor shows where the alcoholic just so happens to be a badass surgeon and he's about to do an open-heart number. I sure hoped that wasn't about to happen because my stomach was already doing somersaults from the smell of grape sulfur. That's exactly what that damned room smelled like, grape sulfur.

Yes, let's not open anything (or anyone, for that matter) today.

***

There was a weird sense of relief that I felt while gazing at the dead. She was blue. I was relieved that out of all the people I knew across Echodale, this one was taking me a while to recognize. My biggest fear at that moment was that they would pull back that sheet and it would be an old friend, or a business partner. One of those janky club promoters that may have made one too many bad deals. I just didn't want to see or feel anything like that. The red lotus emerged from the shadows. She always finds solace in the corners of rooms until she decides to lead them. It was the red dress today, by the way.

She walked out and raised her finger slowly, twirling it counterclockwise, graceful as jazz. The detectives were looking at me, I could feel them. The doctor was flipping through pages on a clipboard next to Jane Doe. The red lotus just kept twirling that finger. I felt that she was signaling me to walk around the body. Telling me to get loose and not to be afraid. You wouldn't hear it but I heard that. All in that beautiful finger of hers. I obliged that finger and shuffled around the body.

"So, not next of kin, eh?" said Detective flunkie. I do enjoy sarcasm.

She was mixed with a few cultures and I could tell she was peaceful before her last breath. It was just all around her. If we weren't standing in that room full of frozen drawers, I actually may have thought that she was just sleeping. In blue paint, of course. Then she disappeared back under the oversized white sheet.

The lead detective spoke, "Listen, uh… why don't you, uh, ping us if you can think of anything. W'could use whatever you have. Sorry to waste your time, Kid."

***

It was a weird moment, man. Very important for the rest of what I'm going to tell you today, though. I thought about it for a long time after leaving the frozen drawers and that beautiful unknown lady. That night, I was going to take Derry across the border to see Armonti play against Toronto. Well, I shouldn't say "was" because we did go. I just wasn't all the way there because my mind was still at Galloway.

***

One thing became very apparent since my years at State: Armonti Perry was destined to be a star. If you remember, bringing him onto our team ruffled a lot of feathers because sometimes that is what greatness does. It takes a little while for everyone around the shining star, the other planets in the atmosphere, to align themselves according to the new sun. Think about it like this, if something changes with our sun, something would shift in the rest of the planets (including ours). I wasn't mature enough to realize that when we welcomed Perry to the team. He was so good and so young, I think my ego just wanted to put him in his place, if you will. Even while I was in Germany and he got that first big contract, I shouldn't have reacted the way I did. I should have just been happy to be a part of his journey. I was immature and egotistical but once I began to shed those characteristics and started accepting my new life, I began to enjoy Perry's journey. He appreciated me for that, too.

"Dio! Even better in person," Derry kept cheering next to me. "Dio! Dio!"

Poor old man. He wanted to jump up and run around but even walking was a struggle for him. He's a good man, though. You know that. He never let the circumstances limit him. I think he was so happy to wake up after surgery that finding something to smile about was not difficult for him. It was fun (and exhilarating) watching Derry enjoy that Seattle-Toronto game. Perry was putting on a show and we were just two rows up from the floor; right in the action.

"Ay, man. Go get'cho sneakers," he yelled from the floor during a free throw.

THE OTHER BLUE

"All I got is dress shoes tonight, Monti."

37 points. That kid scored 37 points against the hottest team in the league at the time. That's when Toronto won four titles in like a five-year span, or something crazy like that. Do you remember? Seattle was good but Perry hadn't gotten them to the championship yet. He was on the brink of history that year though, on the path to becoming the youngest player to ever hit 10,000 career points. What a kid.

We were buried in popcorn as the stands emptied after the game. Derry was so excited (and couldn't run around like he wanted to) that he was flinging popcorn everywhere all night. There was one that slid down my shirt, man. I couldn't help but smile as I fished it out. I realized it was the first time Derry had really experienced American professional hoops in person. He was excited and when you love someone, their excitement is really your excitement.

"So, let me... Help me understand, lefthand," Derry began. "Penny, Perry, Arrington, Pittman... All of you. Same team?"

"Same team."

He just shook his head. The spirit of the game robbed him of maturity and replaced it with a boy-ish sense of curiosity. Just like kids counting the stars, trying to make the night sky seem possible.

"You're Austin Arrington," a smiling teen walked down to us. "Whoa! I knew it! I knew it! 'AP' kept talking to you guys… I- I swear I knew it!"

"You're right, kid! Wassup wit'chu?"

"We've got to take a picture, bro. I've been watching your film, like- this is insane," he replied.

"Oh yeah? You hoop, bro?" I asked after the selfie (Derry's leg was in the shot, too).

"I'm a combo. At…at Terry Prep. It's up here in the city. Up by the water, " he said.

His love for the game was oozing like a freshly popped zit.

"Not a lot of clock right now, though. That's why I've been studying so much. My dad brought me to the game to see it up close," the kid continued.

He pointed to his dad and I gave him a hero's salute. Good men know the value of moments like these and believe in how they inspire us. A lot of times those same good men are inspired by their failed dreams. The silver lining is understanding how important inspiration is. If it doesn't make sense, it will when you're a father.

"How old are you?"

"15, today, sir."

"15 playing varsity? Oh yeah, you've got the juice," I patted his shoulder. *"Just be patient and keep giving it your all. When some of those big guys graduate, you'll be next up. Stay ready. 'Got me?"*

"Yeah, take that advice, kid. He's part of the reason I'm out here now," Perry said creeping into the scene.

He was being swallowed by an oversized royal blue blazer, resting on top of a black turtleneck and a skinny gold chain. His black slacks swallowed his legs. Only the shiny tips of his shoes were exposed.

The boy lost it, "AP!"

They took pictures as Perry stood in the tunnel. You probably could guess that Derry wanted some pictures as well. I promised the kid I would stay in touch so we connected on one of those apps before they left. I got the father's information too. Then it was just the three of us standing (and sitting) in the arena.

"Y'know what I need, man? I need that move you would do on the baseline," Perry spoke with an eyebrow raised.

"Man, you've been talking about that since college but still ain't come to the gym to get it," I barked.

We shared a laugh, the same one we shared for years. It was always about that one move on the baseline. Truth be told, he wanted it because he could never stop it. But that's another conversation for another set of beers. What Perry said next is what really told me that our relationship was valued.

> "Well listen," he started, "I've got cleared to stay a few days. Thought it'd be good to hang out with you. Catch up, a bit."

Derry's smile was loud and silent. I knew that on the inside he had become a toddler.

> *"Really? They 'lettin you stay in town?"*

He replied, "Yes sir!"

> *"Lan Se Huayan!"*

"What?" Perry laughed.

> *"It's my favorite spot for grub up here. Open all night, man. You won't believe it. Food's crazy! Low key, too."*

Just like that, I felt like a kid who was about to have a sleepover. Those Friday nights where my mom would allow my best friend, Eddie, to come spend the night. We'd stay up in basketball shorts and tank tops, playing games until the sun came up. Then we'd play some more and fall asleep on our pancakes; snoring and making bubbles in the syrup. Those were the days. Friendship always feels good, no matter the age.

Perry laughed some more. He could tell we were excited.

"Cool with me, man. Meet me out in the visitor's gate. I'got a rental," he walked off like a rich pastor.

It was a beautiful sports car, lime green and really shiny. I wasn't into cars yet but this was the beginning of it. I couldn't believe that it was a rental. I thought all rentals were those awkward family cars and the occasional V6 sports cars. That's when I decided that I wanted a two door. It wasn't too popular of an idea with a baby on the way but I didn't think it would be too painful of a decision. Especially because Deja was completely enamored with SUVs. Anyways, sorry about the tangent. That car was special. Now, onto the restaurant.

***

"Sometimes it's love and sometimes it's witchcraft," Perry said at the table.

I noticed his empty ring finger as he was helping himself to the fresh pot of Lo Mein.

He continued, "the last one got me for 17 mil. But at this point, shit, what can you do?"

"-love is worth it," Derry said.

It was one of those bold statements that kind of paused the room. At least it felt like it. It definitely caught Perry by surprise. His eyes said so.

"Yeah?" Perry asked.

Derry's confidence was growing steady. I let these two gentlemen talk and get more acquainted because, well, onion soup is my favorite. It was piping hot, too. Just sitting in front of us, begging for attention. I figured I'd handle the needy soup and let them discuss love, or whatever they were talking about.

> "You know," Derry began with one leg hunched over the other, "I was married once. Grande'. Grande'! Grande' Amore! It was real. Once you get a taste of that, and know it exists, si? Well, just keep fighting, lefthand."

Perry knew that Derry's words were honest and deep. The kind of words that make you silent while you finish making your plate of asian cuisine.

> "Noted. If I have any money left, I'll keep trying," Perry said.

> Derry smiled, "love can save your life, don't give up."

We took a few minutes to enjoy a few bites. Well, they were trying to catch up to me. I was already making love to the plate. I had a feeling that Perry was playing some sort of charade that night. Not anything nefarious or mischievous but more so, I don't know; equivalent to playing dumb. Innocence, I suppose. I was right. When he finally took off his mask and embraced Derry, my Italian friend became as light as a corner of a shredded love letter.

THE OTHER BLUE

Perry spoke (after his big disgusting gulp of calamari), "you know, Miercone'. It's good to see you here on our side of the world, man."

Derry's face lit up. Come on, you know it feels good to be recognized. That ounce of joy you get when you see a neighbor in the grocery store. Or, that fun feeling of someone recognizing you by your social handle. He melted into Perry's aura. Remember, Derry was a huge hoops fan and for that period of the game, Armonti Perry was pretty much the best in the world. He knew Derry and well, you get it.

He replied, "Ah, Si, Si. Paradise didn't need me anymore. After-"

"Man, what about Steckler?" an inquisitive Perry asked, "I guess, h- how did you - hm, Ok. What was your secret?"

It was refreshing to see Perry lose his words. I thought it was a sham at first, but then I noticed that he really did have respect for the man. Derry has really done some remarkable things.

"You see, lefthand, it's n'much of a secret a'tall. It's just love. Amore'. Like I told this one here, it's love. I loved to win so I cherished the process of winning. I loved my teammates; ask this one, lefthand. He's even met one, si? I- I loved those guys so I cherished getting to know them, si? I cherished knowing what it means for them to win, si? Knowing what it took.

And of course, I loved my wife," he paused. "I cherished making her proud and worked hard to provide for her. It's not a secret, my boy."

I nodded my head and so did the last of my onion soup going down my throat.

"This is my guy, right here," I assured Perry about Derry.

"Mine too, now," he responded, "I needed that." "So Austin, wassup, man? What's been going on?"

I hate that question, honestly. It always feels like I have an answer for it until someone asks it. The curse of entrepreneurship...newfound entrepreneurship. Sometimes I wanted to respond, *I don't know, you tell me.*

But I said, *"well. Just quit the radio gig a few weeks ago. A station down in Echodale. Uh, getting this business off the-"*

He bit, "business, what kind of business?"

"Well...It's media. Production, web de-"

"Ok, listen," he leaned up in his chair, over the last dumpling, may I add. "Who'your bank?"

"My... bank?"

"Yeah, FirstFi? Blanks?" he persisted.

THE OTHER BLUE

I'm FirstFi..."

"Ok," he responded while he fiddled on his phone.

Derry looked at me and I looked back at him. We both were swimming in confusion.

"Why you ask, bro? You good?"

Just as I finished my sentence I got a notification from my bank that $20,000 had been sent to my account. Twenty. Thousand. Dollars. My tongue was trying to count the money and was too busy to find the words. I kept staring at my phone and Derry didn't say a word. He did smile a little bit, as if he was familiar with the gesture. I had been reminded that he too was a man of wealth. I looked back over to Perry who had been ambushed (a little dramatic) by our waitress, the owner, and two other servers, trying to take a picture for the wall.

"Monti, what's this?" I asked while he was smiling at the staff. He finished up with them before turning back to me, "I need a favor, bro. I think you guys can help me."

***

He went on about a documentary project he wanted to start. His passion was becoming what we see today; the kids, the homes and all of that. He wanted to highlight his journey from the group home to the big leagues. I won't lie, he's always been sort of a workhorse. Definitely stayed in the gym as much, if not more than me and GP back in the day. He wanted to share how important that mindset was to building the man that he became. I just wish he would've asked if it was something we could do first before sending me the money. It was just a weird feeling of good (and green) pressure.

"Perry, come on. What's this?"

He asked, "let's do it. Whatever you need, just let me know. I mean, sounds like that's ya'thing."

"Pe-"

"Bro, just take a few days and look up some stuff. I'll circle back with you when I get back to Seattle. Probably like next week. We'll get it worked out," he affirmed.

Derry smiled. He had the eyes of a father.

I said (with a broken tongue - it was still counting the money), *"I don't even know what just happened."*

"Well, pardon me. I'could be wrong, left hand, but it sounds like your company just got its first cient," Derry said as he waived the waiter down.

I chuckled a little bit. I think he was right. It was weird because I didn't think too much about playing basketball anymore. I always struggled with seeing Perry's success, you know that. It wasn't anything personal. It was just difficult for me to realize that I wasn't a failure just because I hadn't succeeded like him (in basketball). You would think that this moment would be a bit overwhelming but for whatever reason, I actually felt some comfort. I think it was more so just a good evening with good people. Another side of the surreal feeling that I thought professional sports would give me. It kind of charged me up.

I smiled and said, *"let's do it!"*

The joyous moment put me on its wings and carried me to the heavens. Not to mention, the onion soup was so good, too. It was just a good night. The waiter returned and I took care of the bill (figured it was the least I could do at this point). She walked away with a hefty $700 (USD) tip from Mr. Armonti Perry. Her smile was too heavy for her to carry, honestly. I could see it even when she turned her back. But when she turned back around, my heart dropped. She had the face of the Jane Doe from earlier at Galloway.

I jumped.

Then, the rest of the faces in the restaurant became her and they all stared at me, desperate for my attention. I knew that we had to leave. I had to get back to the states.

7 THANK GOD FOR DEJA

Those faces followed me for days. Armonti stayed in Toronto that night but we caught up just before he flew back to the west coast. Come to find out, his $20,000 project was something I actually could handle. I'd done it on the side when I first began working in the media (since my basketball dreams had officially dribbled away - out of bounds, they dribbled out of bounds). It's just that I had done it for far cheaper. He wouldn't accept my discount, though. Especially after learning that Deja was pregnant. That's when I began working on the "Perry Tales" documentary. It was Impact's first major work, but most people don't know that it was my first professional one. Keep in mind, I had only been away from basketball for a year. Maybe closer to two, actually.

***

Those days after meeting with Armonti were tough. Home was taxing and the rent was always due. It was suffocating at times. She was pregnant and I was immature, an ever-dangerous potion of explosive proportions. We had a moment by our bay window that told me she was worth it (yeah, I was that immature…the baby bump wasn't enough). You see, most people don't know that Deja is really the one who made "PerryTales" happen. That sports acumen and energy has been part of her identity. She used to glow on those sidelines while we were chasing trophies at State. She enjoyed the game and she learned to enjoy telling the game's stories even more.

You can't forget when…
They have to hear about…

THE OTHER BLUE

Did you put in…?

She rotated between those statements 4 times an hour, each day during the project. As consistent as your local train headed downtown. If it misses a day of work, well, you know how costly it is to miss your train to work. We've all been there. This was no different because it was those persistent (and "naggy") questions that helped shape that thing. It's a significant part of Armonti's story, today. She knew that was going to happen and that's why she never let me quit.

> *"-ugh, fuck this,"* I said as my head fell to the countertop.

> "Whoa. Ok, one; the mouth. Do something about that," she replied, "love." "Two; why are you giving up? Huh? Wass'wrong?"

She rested her (huge) head in her hand and tilted it with a sarcastic smile. One of those awkward looks that felt passively inviting. Those same eyebrows my mom would use when she was putting her foot down. The kind you only want to make proud. There was no other choice. That's why I only pulled my head up for a quarter of a second before burying my face in the counter.

> "Wass'wrong?" She persisted.

> *"I'm just tired."*

> "Ok, can you lift your head up and talk to me?"

My neck cranked up. It was slow, dramatic, and even came with a loud sigh.

> *"I should give him the money back," I whined, "just...call Kevin and let him do it. I'm over it."*

"Kevin. Baby-"

> *"No, seriously. Like, all of this, " I said while flipping through my scribbled and scrabbled notepad, "what even is this?" "We haven't even started shooting, yet. How the-"*

"Stop, stop, just stop all of that. Just- no," she said while waddling over to the kitchen, "I don't know why but this is making me upset and I didn't want to get upset."

I got up from the counter because I thought it was hubby-duty time but-

"No. Sit down and don't move," Deja barked.

She didn't even look at me. In fact, she wasn't looking at anything. She was kinda just staring into the hallway, it was to my left. You know what, though? I sat down and didn't move. You listen to a pregnant lady, you hear me?

> "-now, I'm sorry, ok?"

> *"-baby, you don't have-"*

"I just… I don't know why you are talking like this. I don't want to do this again. I'm tired, babe. I'm tired, ok? I'm tir- Just- I just want you to see you the way I've always seen you. Ok? The champion. The star… you never see it and I'm tired of that. Just - I don't know, Austin." "You ever think that maybe it's supposed to be difficult? It wasn't easy to beat Carolina, right? You did… so… so much to win that game, honey. You made it happen. Even after all you went through… We…. Like, for us. Why don't you see this?"

I tried to get back up, *"baby…"*

"No. I'm not done," she waved that infamous pointer finger. "You have to learn to stop giving up. It's…it's heavy. Ok? You're ok, you're where you need to be. Can we just be great?"

She finally let me stand but I didn't have anything to say. My arms did the talking as they wrapped around her.

***

The rest of the night was about the other lady in my life. She was wearing a red leather one piece skirt set (I forgot what you call them). Her words were never really words and they surely weren't gentle. I stayed up scribbling storyboards in my notebook and she would just sit there, giggling at me. She would only do it when I stopped writing, though. My most vulnerable moments. I realized the relationship between the two after a few hours and decided to keep my head down, to keep working, you know?

"The girl," she whispered into my ear.

"-*ah*,"

"Sorry, didn't mean to scare you, baby," Deja said from the threshold.

I turned over my shoulder, *"you'good, you'good. You didn't scare me."*

She slipped into the shadows, leaving her trace of love. That woman is, was, and always will be my everything. I waited for her footsteps down the hall and into the bedroom. I never heard the door close, though. It's fine. I just needed some space (and time) to get to working on another project.

8 THIS ISN'T BASKETBALL

I called it *Project Cold Wednesday*. Don't ask why because I literally have no idea where the title came from. I was very public about my work, with family and friends, even in the early days. But, I kept 'PCW' very close to my chest. Mainly because it was dealing with a real dead body and dead bodies are always inte-... uh, serious.

The key to smiling is finding a lesson in the painful moments. It's a realization that life is going to happen (well, death in this particular instance) and that challenges will arise. The better part of me, the beginning of my fortune that you've come to witness for the last half-century, began with the understanding that everything poses an opportunity to learn something. Those lessons are sometimes the prize and always are available. Even in your pain, you can learn something from it. I tell you this because that's why I couldn't stop thinking about Jane Doe. I felt that there was some sort of opportunity in accidentally being dragged into that cold room. The red lotus must have thought so too. She led me to it. You know? It couldn't have been for no reason. Very few things are actually pointless. I took that energy and made something of it. Jane Doe's cold face was going to haunt me every single day if I hadn't.

***

We were just a few weeks into Impact's conception and I had two major projects on the stove. Perry Tales and PCW. I couldn't explain the thinking, but I just knew that if both of them became successful, it would set us up for a bright future. I'm getting carried away, sorry about that. Let me-

***

One night, Deja had been asleep for a few minutes before I started working on PCW. Or, at least she was quiet enough for me to think she was asleep. I started locally, right there in Echodale. I looked around all of the records of missing people to see if I could draw any conclusions. I started describing what I could remember about that face - the wide eyes, heavy eyebrows, high cheekbones. Whatever I could think of from those few moments I spent with Jane Doe. I reimagined myself in that room and watched the red lotus direct me around the body. That's when I remembered an angel's kiss above her left ear. It was just like mine, actually. I used to stick earrings (sometimes, more dangerous items) in there when I was a kid. Legend has it, we're "special" people who can see the dead. It holds some sort of veil, I think. Look it up. That's true.

"Austin, babe. You coming to lay down?"

"Shit," I jumped.

She replied, "wass - wass'wrong? You ok?"

"I'm fine, you just scared me, baby. I'll be in there like...Give me a few minutes, ok?"

She yawned. It was one of the toddler-esque yawns. It was cute.

"Ok, just hurry up. I need the arms," she charmed.

The pregnant lady was light on her feet, man. She would glide all over that apartment and never make a sound. Looking back, I don't know why I was so nervous about her finding out about 'PCW'. I probably could have used her help. Some of it may have been because I don't think she would want me investigating a murder. I didn't want to either but I wanted Impact Communications to be the first to report on it. Sacrifice. It's in the bible, you know?

***

None of the missing persons reports seemed familiar. You probably could have guessed that. The police would have cracked that mystery quickly. I fell back into that old wooden chair we had (it was our early, young, "cheap furniture" days). Just couldn't get that lady's face out of my head. She followed me as I walked around the room, turning out the lights and shutting off the computer. I was walking out and heard the red lotus's bangles jingling. They were syncopated beats, too. Could have made a song from them.

Jane Doe's face kept me up that night and honestly, it was then when I decided that I would begin Impact.world (we just hit 2 billion subscribers... thank you!). Whatever I discovered would need a place to be reported and plus, I loved to write. I thought it would be great to have a place where Impact could publish its own editorial pieces and help others in the process. I'm sure you know, but even Deja started writing for it. That wasn't until later though. We had moved to Montana Bay by then. But the initial idea for the site came to me as I laid in bed that night with Deja in my arms and Jane Doe in my eyes.

***

"..It's a beautiful city, left hand, it really is," Derry said to me, a few days later, under that big Oak tree you see on the news all the time. The pride of Echodale. "But, I come here… To the states. I want to see them. At least another."

"Derry, I understand. Really, I do. I mean, Deja's working-"

"But it won't be soon, or anything. Still need to get my feets," he continued.

You should have seen him sliding down in his chair. I don't think he even realized he was doing it. Honestly, he was practically on the floor. My eyes danced into the horizon and my empty face was their stage.

"-ah," Derry exclaimed, "what is it, my boy? That look." He did a gesture with his hands over his face, his elbow knocking over his water. "I'm sorry, I'm sorry," he continued while cleaning up his mess. I picked up my phone so it wouldn't drown in the puddle.

"-it's a cold wednesday, Derry. I just feel a little…Cold."

His bottom lip stuck itself out, propelled by disgust and firmness.

"Eh-eh, cold? This," Derry said with a hand in the air, "ah, left hand. Sure."

He chuckled and got up to throw away the napkins from his crime scene. He was struggling though. That was one of the moments when I realized Derry's condition after the fall. I had a tendency to forget that night in Paradise but seeing him move so gingerly was a reminder.

"Let me take it."

"No, lefthand. If… you.. Ugh," he replied while fighting to stand, "er-… help me. Then, well… How will I- help me?"

Two people you don't argue with: the pregnant and the elderly. The longer you live, the longer that list gets, you know? But I let Derry fight his own battle and get himself to that trashcan and back. Plus, it gave me time to find the words to say. I really didn't want to pretend as if my mind was clear. Derry has always been a good friend to me, well, since we met in Paradise. His wisdom and endearment has been a guiding light. A compass, if you will.

My face twisted up on its own, *"Derry, listen bud,"* I said as he returned after a few years of walking. *"There's no lying to you, bro. You know me-"*

"That, I do."

"I'm stressed, man. That's probably what you see. It's not the the, uh- you know, normal stress, either. Like, don't be worried about me, or anything. I'm just in foreign territory. My life is foreign right now, for real."

"You and me both, lefthand. I knew something was up. Look at that chicken, you barely ate!"

The Chicken always tells the story. Not to be racist, or anything. Let's move on.

He continued, "you'might need some time, lefthand. Just a few hours, if you can. Alone- Maybe, basketball or something on the telly."

"I have a pregnant wife, remember?"

"She's still working though. When Sienna was still in that phase, lefthand…She'd leave and I took time for me, you know, yeah?"

I shook my head, *"yeah. I hear you."*

"I mean, here it is, lefthand. You've only got a little time before she's not working anymore. Then you really will be choked on the bell," he said pointing to his watch. Actually, he was tapping the hell out of that watch.

"Well, when she's gone, I'm working- trying to make Impact into something. It's…Well,"

He interjected, "damn work! You'mericans, all you know is work. They turn you'to machines n'you just go, go, go. All the money, no life. A pity."

He had a point but you know Uncle Sam couldn't care less about his soliloquy. In this country, you get rich or die trying (while making someone else rich). It's kind of hard to tell a rich person that but we were in two different classes.

I didn't get all of this, yet. I was working toward it though.
That was the point.

> *"Well, maybe I shouldn't have left RUMBLE. You know?*
> *That's what's - weighing me down, a bit. I've got to put food*
> *on that table."*

He slammed his cup down, "but'who's going to do it
if you die trying? Eh?"

Some other people eating at the Oak tree looked
over. It kind of startled me, too. It was a fair point. I think it
was actually worthy of that hard cup-slamming and it would
have been even better if there was some thunder behind his
voice. Maybe even a streak of lightning.

> "Let me help you, lefthand. I've got a few
> tomorrow's left and you know how much- how
> much…Well, how well I do things. Very detailed.
> You know I love you like a son and only want what's
> best. Let me help, lefthand."

> *"Well, I don't see why-"*

> "Plus," he interjected, "It'll give me something to do.
> Feel'like my days are just sunrises, this stuff (pointing
> to the food) and sunset. I miss Paradise Cove."

> *"The Cove? Or, Steckler?"*

"Italy," he affirmed. "The Chariot. All of it. You know, I'm not one to'be...uh, still. I've been loving it here but...Very still. Ver'scary."

We shared a moment of eye-tango. Our souls shook hands through our pupils, way before we even spoke. Truth be told, Derry has been a partner of mine since we first met. But, you know that. He's always been someone I could lean on so we really didn't need an agreement or this borderline-erie conversation. I did wish that I had just been more direct about needing help in the first place. I probably wouldn't have run myself down like that if I had gone into Impact with help.

"Derry, you know you're my guy, right?"

He smiled before sipping his tea. "So, this means I have a job?"

"It's you and me, bro."

He sipped his tea again and the clouds behind him began hugging each other. Call me crazy, but they actually slid out of view and made room for the beaming winter sun. It's almost as if it knew it weren't going to be out too long so it made sure it shined its brightest on us that day. Derry had been close but that day, he became everything. Blood couldn't make us any closer. I always appreciated his humility, too. His riches never got in the way of helping me discover mine. A true angel and a friend.

"I'm excited, lefthand," he continued. "What are you working on? H'many on the table?"

I looked away, *"only one, right now. The Perry Tales project with Armonti. It's- some sort of, uh, streaming deal on the table so he's really pressing about it. That's all I've got, right now."*

***

Our routine was to get together every weekday morning at 7:30. He'd bring coffee to the house and we'd walk around the room, barking ideas at each other. Things evened out over time as he started to assist me instead of trying to dominate the projects. It's tough when you have two, what they call, "alpha" personalities. Our relationship being so strong has always kept us on the straight and narrow, though. We may have squabbled about ideas but we found our way to reconciliation. He continued to offer just enough resistance to my thoughts to keep things fresh. It helped a lot with *Perry Tales* because man, it just got stale. It was one of those things that I agreed to for the coin but my heart wasn't in it. There was a little tension, too.

***

Kevin Crumb was a local videographer who I met while on the club circuit in Echodale. He's one of those types of associates that we add on in adult life, the ones who we wouldn't choose to spend time with but wouldn't die if we had to. He also was the first person I thought about when it came to video production of any kind, even before *Perry Tales*. We'd done a few small projects together by then. Things like social media videos and highlights of me at various events in the city. This was definitely the biggest project we'd done together.

"-Derry, just…. Hold on for a second, bud," Kevin exclaimed through the screen. "Let me just sort this out with Austin, here… What about that?"

"Lefthand, ugh… The devil of time, this one!" Derry said as he marched off into the hallway.

I didn't like that.

"Derry, wait…" He went into the other room. *"Kevin… Are you… good? Man."*

He replied with eyes looking off screen, "I'm fine. That guy, man. I just can't deal."

"But…Derry is one of the best guys I know. Family, for real. I just don't understand y'all issues."

Derry barged back in, "that one's lazy! Lumaca! Lumaca! See'more go in a dead horse."

"We don't understand you, old man!" Kevin said off camera (note: virtual teamwork kind of makes the dream work).

"Well, wait… Hold on, guys. What-"

Derry interjected, "This! Just add that photo n'stop the drag…that lazy! It's a disease!"

"It doesn't need to be there!" Kevin shouted. "You're just trying too hard, old man. Let us take care of this n'you just take care of the coffee!"

He hadn't come back to the camera, yet.

"Kevin!"

He came back to the camera with a sandwich hanging from his lips like a window-washer hanging from the side of the building. His beard was decorated with ham and cheese. He was chewing loud enough to wake the neighbors. Mrs. Dortch and those damn cats. I was so frustrated.

"Listen!... What- what photo? Show me the picture... Derry!" I thought he had walked back into the hallway (I would have after hearing that god-awful chewing sound).

"Here, lefthand," the old man said over my shoulder, "it's this one. Remember this?"

I did. It was a photo of me and Perry holding each other at half court with National Championship hats on. There was confetti everywhere but it never covered our smiles. Nothing could. Those tears of joy were deep enough to swim in and the world was ours.

Of course I remembered that.

"One of my favorites, man. Where was this going to go?"

Derry responded, "well, I think… There's - some point in that script'where he talks about you. He goes on about what you did and… I just thought-" There was a twinkle in his eye.

Kevin (ham-sammich boy) interjected, "it's just not needed! I've already got the b-roll of that night. Ev-even like, little clips of you."

"The boy talks about you and you're not on the screen!" Derry replied. "Not even the right timing-ugh, lefthand. You should see-"

I couldn't take it anymore, *"tell you what. Send me the file, Kevn. I'll look and decide what to do."*

He didn't like the authoritative response but I'm sure he liked the idea of him not having to do any more work. It was written all over his face with that mustard around his mouth. I knew Derry meant well and I wasn't playing favorites, either. It really was a good picture. It did make a lot of sense for it to be spliced into the video at that point because it really highlighted our relationship and the impact it had on his career - even if it was a still shot instead of a video. Damn good observation by Derry but Kevin didn't have the heart to be corrected. Humility isn't for everybody. I knew that going in, though. I shouldn't have worked with him.

***

Majority of our days were just like that. It would be extremely peaceful and productive until we got on the call with Kevin about the editing and shooting. There were the occasional days that they didn't bicker but most of the time I was caught in the middle like a teenage son in an abusive home, protecting his mother. One day (about a week later) we got a call that shook the routine.

***

"I'm pulling it, Austin," Perry said over the screen. "Keep the money, 'don't care about that. But... yeah, this is done."

Derry got up from his favorite wicker chair, confused and alarmed.

"Lefthand," he pleaded his way into the camera, "what's the pickle here? Wass'wrong, lefthand?"

"We just need to pause things for a little while," Perry said with eyes to the ground.

I hadn't seen him like this before. Well, he was in a similar state at GP's homegoing service but, you get the point. Something was eating away at the All-Star.

"-Let's take a few... Get back on things a lil'later," he continued.

He didn't leave room for a response and rushed off the call like a dishonest Mayor. I was glad he didn't ask for the money back because that's what I had been surviving off of. Derry wouldn't let me pay him because he's still filthy rich (even 'til this very moment - filthy rich, I tell you). It was a weird feeling, though. I had actually become invested in Perry Tales. More invested after that small altercation between

Derry and Kevin. I'll say that Derry really brought some joy to the entire experience and shed light on the dark spot of the project - Kevin. I was enjoying working with Derry and I feared that we'd have nothing else to work on, you know? It didn't matter though.

'Armonti Perry has ended the call.'

9 A PERFECT JAWLINE

Time escaped me. Deja's gyno had the ugliest office in New York. Everything was blue and loud. The wallpaper was like black licorice in a chocolate factory. I hated it but this is where Deja was comfortable. Happy wife, happy... you know the rest. Probably won't say that again, either.

'Doctor Shabby' did have quite the collection of Rubik's Cubes. I sat there twiddling away, looking back and forth at Deja to see if she saw me being a badass. You know, Rubik's Cubes are turn ons. She always sat there so calm and cheery. Her legs were usually crossed and her stomach was always smiling. I watched it with all the love in my body. That's when I felt a breeze over my shoulder. It wasn't a draft or anything, 'Doctor No-Taste' was on the 9th floor.

I kissed the draft back and that's when I saw her. The red lotus. Her stomach was smiling too. I looked back at Deja and then back at the lotus, she was in fact, with child. My beard dragged across that hideous carpet. I turned back to the Rubik's Cube with a nervous focus that prompted my wife's usual, *are you okay?*

Yeah, hon. I'm fine.

I couldn't even explain it to myself. All I had was that beautiful Cube to help sort out my nervous energy. It was as vibrant as a theme park's horizon. As electric as a frayed lamp wire, swimming in a puddle.

***

There he was, 'Dr. Not-Martha-Stewart', standing in the doorway. His hands were huge like mine and his bone structure was defined. Chiseled - godly. I was a little bit taller. It was like staring at myself today, back then. Anyways, that's not important.

"Deja, this is exciting isn't it?" 'Dr. Me' said.

She responded, "yes, it is! We are… Just… Can't believe this is really happening, you know?"

Her eyes were in mine and her hand was on my thigh. My nervous smile is hideous so I won't make you think about it. Unless you're doing that now. Then, my bad.

I warmed her heart, "yeah, baby. This is what we've been praying for."

It calmed me. Helped me ignore my other pregnant bride. I meant it, too. It was an exciting time for us and words couldn't describe the feeling of becoming a dad for the first time.

"-Well, that's just nice. Austin, always good to see you, my friend. We miss hearing you everyday," 'Dr. Perfect' said.

"Well," I laughed nervously, "I'm still here, doc. Feels good to be missed. That life was a lot though."

"- He's been a lot lighter since RUMBLE," Deja said while rubbing my thigh. "Happier, too."

"It's just a tough industry," I rested my words on the room. Thought I was in therapy for a second.

'Dr. Jawbone' smiled, "agh. Son, after all we've seen you do… You can do it all. You will, too. Deja, come on back when you're ready."

He disappeared down the hall and my bride soon followed. They left me with the red lotus and the doctor's loving words which I appreciated dearly.

***

There we were. Me and the red lotus, just sitting there trying not to draw attention to ourselves. I struck up this weird conversation with the receptionist about ice cubes. She probably wanted to drug test me but was too shy. I believe experts would call that situation 'word-vomit'. I was puking everywhere and the lotus was just stroking the back of my head like a proud mom during counseling. That mom who always thought her "baby" was special, no matter how many 4th place plaques were on the wall.

Thankfully, 'Dr. Perfect' summoned me to his lair - I mean, office. He pushed the door open and Deja's eyes were pink and ripe. My face and my heart slid down my throat like a splattered egg on a window.

"Oh, no. Honey… Wha-wass'wrong?"

She sniffled, fighting the tears that were choking her.

"Huh? Wass'wrong?" I continued as I got closer, rubbing my hand across her crown.

Deja didn't want to talk but 'Dr. Bone Structure' had to. That was literally his job. I looked at him with questions in my eyes and silence on my tongue. My eyes slid away for a second at the shadow under the door. I had to regain focus and you know, be strong for Deja. She was losing it and I swore to protect her from losing it. Those vowels were real to me.

He huffed and stood up. "Well, Mr. Arrington," he began. "It seems we've discovered something today. Now, I don't want you two to get worried, or scared- It's... I'm here."

"You're scaring me, doc..."

"No, no, no, seriously," he laughed in a dry tone. "You've got my word and full support.... No need to worry."

I looked at Deja and wiped a tear. She nodded and smiled through the others.

"You two should start planning for two," he said at the monitor.

If confusion had a color, I would have turned that. Deja was too blue to be confused.

"But, how? The gender reveal... I thought we were past all of that..."

"No," he affirmed. As hard as a judge in a steamy romance with their gavel. "This is what I was worried about with missing those appointments - trying to push for the reveal. We've got to, you know, stay on top of things going forward."

He shared the updated sonogram with us and walked us through the two babies.

"I've got no choice but to call this a miracle," he grinned, "see? Look at that…"

Deja's smile became a lot heavier and so did the tears. She was a ball of emotion, a balloon that never stopped expanding. I'd always think it's about to pop but it just keeps on filling up. Poor love, she was so lost and I just wanted to find her.

"Well," I questioned around the room. I may have been trying too hard but that's better than men who do the opposite. *"That's good…right?"*

"In theory, yes," the doctor said before rising again, "but this does change things. Again… Let's go through this, again… Because I need you guys to work with me on this. Very important."

"Uh huh."

"Let's not worry - let's embrace the changes and we'll take it one step at a time. Together," the Doctor continued.

I nodded and agreed. Deja tried to do the same but, you know.

He continued, "our girl here is still working and with the addition of a second child. That complicates things…"

Deja bursts into tears. Drool and slobber everywhere. If we were there another 5 minutes, we would have drowned.

She sobbed, "tell him the rest."

"The rest?"

He huffed. His bottom lip hid between his teeth. His cheekbones throbbed. He shuffled across the room, removing his gloves, trying to make tough words easier. At least, that's how I perceived it.

He tiptoed, "I want her to go see her PCP about her glucose levels. Er, uh… It's time for some blood work anyway, but again…"

"I know, don't worry. That's kind of hard to do right now, you do understand?"

"I do. But like I said earlier, you can do it all," he said in a personal tone.

The words were hidden from my crying bride who probably wouldn't hear them over her tears anyway. It was a 'man to man' moment. Like the ones you experience on a "guy's-only" hiking trip to Cape Dinnias. Deja began gathering her things and even her jacket cried as she slid the zipper to her chin.

> "Hey, uh… Austin," the Doctor said under his breath as we cleared the room. He waved me down. "This is a precaution thing, you know? I… did see some things that just had me questioning, but it's better to know what we're dealing with. The entire way around. Especially with the addition of a well, the addition of a kid… Another mouth to feed."

Wasn't sure if he was joking.

> *"Yeah."*

Dry statements are just as hard for me as they are for the ones I say them to. But sometimes, it's the only way to Paradise.

> "Listen, just be there for her. Th'best you can do, right now. Karen will upload the results from the labs and if I see anything, I'll call," said the doctor, "well, I'll be in touch anyway and we can go from there."

I rested on his words while part of me was wondering where my bride had wandered to.

> "Oh… Son… That Jane Doe needs a name… She's got one, you know?" he continued.

"Hmph?"

"Yeah? What? I…didn't say anything, son," the doctor responded, "did you have a…question for me?"

"Oh, no. I think we're good for now. Thanks for all your help." A handshake. He had my respect. Great guy.

***

Echodale had a beautiful waterfront park but it didn't survive '32. Everything changed in '32. I used to take Deja through that park to get a quick smile when we first lived there. It was called The Randolph and it overlooked Lake Erie. Yachts swarmed the horizon. Watching the moon stare into the lake's mirror was the prettiest thing in the winter. That moon is a perfectionist. Randolph became our safe haven. A necessity more than a desire. We trekked through it on the way home from 'Dr. Sexy'. Deja's eyes were glued to the window. I could hear the sobbing bouncing off of it. I'm an empath, especially for the ones I truly love. Those tears were louder than heavy metal in a thunderstorm.

"…I'm scared, baby. It's ok to be scared, right?" she questioned.

"Girl, you don't need any permission to feel," I said definitively, "but everything you feel, I'm here to feel with you, if that makes sense. We're 'gonna get through this…and… Look, we're having twins! That's what you always wanted!"

Her smile kissed her red eyes.

Then, "but… What if I do have it, babe? I can't stop thinking about'it." I had those eyes, I really did. Then they left me again. They went looking out of that window trying to find something else to lean on. My shoulder made too much sense. "Like, this could be dangerous, Austin."

I pulled over.

"Stop. No more. We will face it together and I don't want you to think otherwise. Y'know what you got right here." I gently caressed her cheek, "and I know what I have… Now, let Bell know what's going on. - 'Think you should go on Maternity and let's just focus on this together."

It was her body. It was her womb that was carrying the children. It was her stomach that was hanging out of those pants that she hated. It was her back that was paining her to sleep at night and it was her mind that was trying to deal with it all. I never forgot that and that's key to learning how to love someone. The weirdest thing about it is that I felt that it was out of some sort of self-love; a true respect for myself as a man. Honoring my vowels. She's a forever subscriber to the best of me and that's what she got in those words. They were short and sweet instructions but a lot of times, that's all people want. Words they can trust.

That's not for this story, either. That's for you.

Anyway, she began to float. That's when I put my eyes to the rear view mirror and put the car in gear for the journey back home. The red lotus appeared with tears running down her smiling face, her hair disheveled and dull. Her skin was peeling like glue on a kindergartener and her stomach was bulging.

I jumped, *"agh!"* and turned to the back seat.

"Austin! What!" Deja said, also turning around (well, trying to. You know… the belly).

"Nothing, nothing. Ah, - n… nothing a'tall. I'm tweakin'."

10 THE INTERNET MADE ME DO IT

Fridays with maternity-leave-Deja were the best. At least for me. The end of the week was her time to catch up on sleep, for whatever reason. I love my wife dearly but, her sleeping was a break that we both needed. I used Fridays to dive into 'PCW'.

The break in the case came from a Kenlo Online post. I had amassed quite the following after the Paradise fiasco and my Kenlo timeline became my encyclopedia.

I KNOW SOMEBODY SEEN THIS WHITE GIRL, said the post.

It was shared over a million times. The picture was a little dated. Conspiracy-theory comments and flat conversation filled the comment section but it had my attention for hours. I read just about every comment until I got to one from a young lady named Karlie Disquis. She went on to become a doctor, by the way. Damn good one too. Been on TV and everything.

KARLIE: JANE DOE.

That was it. I know you probably were expecting something a little more explosive but…boom. Something about those words dragged my mouse to expand the conversation. Blessings await the curious (among other things).

SEBI SEBI: omg, don't say that. What is wrogn with you???

SEBI SEBI: wrong*

EMMANUEL CLIFFORD: u kno her?

AKOO BRADLEY: Nobody does, apparently.

MAJAH: But somebody has too…

AKOO BRADLEY: You would think that but here we are.

AKOO BRADLEY: Bet this will be one of the gone girl nationwide searches.

KARLIE: Last time anyone has seen her. bailentimes.us/local/bpdtips/chelseasignore-missing-persons

I followed the link to an article about the missing white woman. Her name was Chelsea Signore. The article was talking about her last known whereabouts; a grocery store where she worked. She looked much older in the surveillance footage but her features were still bold. I leaned in close.

"Hmph."

She rocked on her bow legs when she walked in her khaki shorts and apron, typical clerk attire. So innocent, seriously. I'm not trying to add anything to this. It's just that I remember watching that video, becoming weak at her delicacy. A tender soul. You should have seen her smile as she turned around to help a customer with big, brolic shoulders. They spoke for maybe 5 seconds before he left the view and Chelsea rushed away in the opposite direction as if she was being summoned by her mum. Hurried, measured, and gone forever.

It was the angle that was captivating. The video itself was as simple as I just shared. Nothing more, nothing less. I watched it a few more times. I just wanted to see her face again. It hurt to swim that deep in it. I froze the frame just as she sent the customer on his way. Her eyes were piercing. They were glowing, actually. Lighting a path to him. I felt a chill. His face was familiar.

I fell back in my chair. Not too loud, though. I didn't want to wake my (pregnant) sleeping beauty. My other woman was wide awake. She never sleeps. I looked over at her and she grinned with clenched teeth. Like a toddler fighting diarrhea. It grew wider and wider and wider, leaving happy and entering cynic; psycho… you understand. We stared at each other for what felt like years. My arm hairs stood like the Empire when Vader walks in. They wanted to run but they were stuck with me.

"Austin, what are you looking at? You ok?" Deja said from the hallway. "What?"

"Baby," I said, jumping up to greet her, "you're awake. I'm…I'm good!"

She yawned, "ok." "Hey, can you get him-"

It was that damned cat. Or, one of them, I should say. Mrs. Dortch had one particular cat that always found its way to our door. We started letting him in for some reason. Let this be a lesson for you; habits grow up so fast. His name

THE OTHER BLUE

was Shabazz and he was dramatic as hell. He also owes the landlord a new door. Shabazz Krueger would be fitting.

***

Have you ever been working on a puzzle and you find that piece that you just want to make work? You know it fits but you may have to turn it around a few times. Sometimes you have to walk away and come back to it later. That's how I felt about Jane Doe. It's probably the same feeling that you have, it had to be connected to the Chelsea lady.

Shabazz (Krueger) lept into my lap as Deja poured a glass of water and walked her fine ass back to the bedroom. It was 4:30-dark, nothing too crazy. I stroked the pussy with my mind on a puzzle piece and my eyes to the stars.

-and the red lotus had her's on me.

***

I gave it a few days and let it all marinate. I'm lying. I fantasized about it until I started missing calls and texts. Not from Deja, though. That would be suicide. There was someone who helped me a great deal with all of this, but I can't reveal her name. She's still living and working, you know. We'll call her Detective Apple Pie.

We met at a club I used to host on Main Street a few years prior. It was my first residency while in Echodale. She would come by every Friday at 1:22AM like clockwork. Sometimes she'd bring her friends to party. We always joked about how she found a way to show up at the same time each week. I never knew what she did until we were drinking one night and she confided in me after the club. She had some of those '*I've had a long ass day*' tears in her eyes and well, I was there. Deja loved her.

117

I asked Apple Pie to meet me about PCW.

***

"-I'm nervous," said Detective Apple Pie, "this is…different for you, Mr. Arrington."

"Er, yeah… I think I'm desperate, [redacted]. It's good to see you, though. Uh, damn. What happened?"

She replied with a smile and used all her might to lift her hand, "Man… I've got to stop fighting walls. East side the other day. Long story - "

"Ha. I see."

Her eyebrows sank to match her smirk, "well, damn. I'm fine, thank you for asking. It can't look that crazy…"

"[redacted], you've got that big ass thing on your hand. Like, I know that's heavy…"

She crossed her legs and rested her (clubbed) arm on the shiny combat boot. We spent a few minutes playing catch up. Her son had just started kindergarten and she was as proud as a farmer with the best corn at the market. I told her about her girl, Deja (that's what she said all the time; "that's my girl right there"), and the pregnancy news. She was going to be an aunt to another kid so I figured she should know and get her wallet ready. Everyone spoils your first kid.

"We've got a few minutes and I've got to get back across town, Aus. Wassup?" she said.

"Well... I'm looking for these guys. Detectives, I believe. The-"

She interrupted, "ok. My branch?"

"I think so. I mean, I would assume so. The-"

She interrupted, "What're their names?"

"Eh," I tiptoed. *"Lattisaw and a Mederra."*

Apple Pie looked to the sky as if the clouds were some sort of database. Now that I think about it, there is always some magic happening up there, you know? Those clouds and that blue, it just does something to us.

"Lattisaw and Mederra," she repeated in the right lane. "Hmph. Lattisaw and Mederra." Her tongue kept kicking the inside of her cheek. It was throbbing the side of her face like a bass drum. "-And you'sure they are in my department?"

"Well-"

She interrupted, "Gold Division?"

I waited in case she had some more to say. But, she put a (sexy) cup of coffee to her lips so I figured I'd better strike while I could. You know how conversations with conversationalists can be.

"Well, I don't know, to be honest. They just said they were detectives."

She stared at me and I heard her throat fight with that coffee.

"Lattisaw and Mederra. Detectives." All of sudden, the ground was the database. "What'they look like?"

"I- I can't really describe 'em, to be honest. I mean, the Lattisaw dude was the leader-type. Really int-... Just...forceful?"

She questioned my straining eyes, "like, intense? An intense guy?" (She said it, not me, for the record.)

"Yeah... Just-" Then, I did this gesture with my hands to try and paint the picture. *"The other one was really quiet. I mean, he was taking notes and stuff but he was just -"*

"Like... silenced," she said as if she already knew the answer. "And that was Mederra."

"Oh! You know what? Lattisaw was balding. Like, one of those, 'I should have shaved it all off' situations. And... and... I remember they said they were with EPD."

"Lattisaw and Mederra. EPD... Balding," she repeated into the clouds. "Hmph."

Birds were whistling. I could hear the chill in their voices. Apple Pie hopped up and finished the last of her coffee. I had assumed I should get up, too.

She asked, "and they never gave a division? Gold? Not even... Blue?"

"Agh. I mean, not that I can remember. Feel like I would remember that."

"Yeah, I can't even recall the names," she said, shaking her head. "And if they'detectives, I feel like I would at least know the names... Lattisaw -"

"- and Mederra, yeah." I couldn't stand to hear her repeat it again.

"Well, I've got nothing on that..." she replied. "Lattisaw-"

"...and-"

"Mederra, yes. I tell you what, I'll just look through the system when I get back downtown," she said. She was already starting to walk away. "Yeah, because I'm drawing blanks. Everything's ok?"

She was getting to an uncomfortable distance of having to yell to get your point across.

"Yeah, I'm good! Just text me if you find anything!"
***

121

I was nervous the entire day. Well, from that point on. You hope to get reassurance when you're validating an identity, you know? Especially for a guy like me who, at that time, was seeing a dead girl's face everywhere. Sia spent the majority of the day humming in my ear and it was just adding to the discomfort. Her sarcastic grin only made things worse. Old mayonnaise on a stale sandwich.

***

"Who's texting us?" my inquisitive (and nosy slash lovingly-possessive) wife asked me.

She was snuggled on my lap with her belly to the sky, under her gray wool blanket. Her eyebrows held me at gunpoint.

It was Detective Apple Pie and when I told Deja that, she immediately began to worry. I don't know if it was for my safety or the marriage's. I'll assume it was mine because she never brought it back up. Like, out of self-conscious concern, you know?

All she said was, "uh oh" and turned back to watch *Wringo*.

I glanced at the text. I was so nervous looking back up that I could literally feel my heart running to the bathroom to puke. Sia stood up in disbelief, casting a huge shadow from the corner of the room.

Detective Apple Pie found no one in the EPD database with the last names of Lattisaw or Mederra.

11 NERVOUS, NOT SCARED

But, you knew that already. Everybody sees that one coming. Each time I re-tell that story, it just feels like everyone knew something was off. It never truly made sense. A cold body, two detectives, a wonky doctor, *and me?* When I finally had my first moment on *Late Night with Wringo's* couch, his jokes were all surrounded by the 'duh' aspect of the story. They were pretty good, too. Not good enough for me to remember but I'm sure you've heard a few.

After a few hours, I wrote Apple Pie back. I wanted to wait until my pregnant wife went to sleep because her heightened senses didn't just detect smells and such. She became quite the detective. I was juggling so many thoughts as she laid in my lap that night, I waited until she dozed off to get back to work on *PCW*. I told Apple Pie we needed to meet again. This time, I suggested we meet across the border.

***

"Listen," she said in a dramatic tone.

Imagine one of those big 'boom' sound effects in a movie right before the main character is about to enter the third act.

"Aus… You've got to tell me what's going on," she stared.

She was right. I had to. We spent 40 minutes beating around the bush and after the hassle of crossing the border, I had to deliver on this conversation. I had made it so dramatic and looking back, the drama was warranted. Jane Doe was an actual dead body and those two detectives weren't really detectives. Even if they were, they weren't who they said they were. Drama warranted. My face twisted trying to organize some words. My tongue was running around like a mad man. I had to grab it and calm it down.

"Eh- A few weeks ago I get a call. I'm at home… It's Galloway General…"

She nodded.

"So, they ask me to come down and ID a body-"

"ID a body?" she interrupted.

"Yeah. And it threw me off because I'm like anybody else, you know? I get worried and start like, thinking about everybody…"

She wanted more.

"So, I mean. I end up going down there and that's where I met our two guys. Lattisaw and -"

"Mederra," she affirmed.

"Yeah."

She continued, "-and, was it a body?"

"Yeah. It was a white lady… A real white lady. The doctor was a little out there, too. I mean… If I'm being honest, the whole place'off."

She replied, "Yeah. That's the G… The people down there can be different some days."

***

Boy was she right. That hospital is arguably the best campus in the nation. That new cancer treatment? It originated in Echodale, right out of Galloway. We had moved to Montana Bay by then but, I remember how proud of the city we were when the story broke. But there's a different side of that beautiful building. Some of the smartest doctors in the world eat lunch on one side and on the other? The meanest, nastiest idiots in the galaxy. I know how big the galaxy is and yes, it could sound dramatic at first. But, no. I mean that. Even before my run in with Jane Doe.

***

One time, we did a holiday special with the children's ward. It was really nice. Shade sent us down there every year with toys and money. Duke would DJ in a Santa Claus outfit (mostly instrumentals or that weird kiddy-remix stuff… the ones that substitute the curse words with polite ones that make no sense). The kid that I was with needed a bottle of water. I walked out and saw the nurses scrambling to care for another child. The entire ward seemed like a zoo. It was rather chaotic and it happened so 'all-of-a-sudden'. You really had to watch where you were walking or you might squish a kid. That kind of busy.

Duke, I mean Santa Claus, was really in his bag though. His instrumental and lo-fi mixes were my favorite. He'd scratch the records as if he was on stage at a concert.

I stood in the zoo on my mission for H20. These beautiful (and I do mean stunning) nurses had become wild apes and a few became elephants. I stuck my head back into my kid's room to let the parents know what the hell was going on out there. They were enjoying a family moment while wearing these cheap Christmas hats. They looked up at me with goofy smiles and the kid had a book in her hand.

>*"I'll go down and get some water... - bring up a few bottles. It's a'zoo out here."*

I took the stairs because elevators are elevators. Plus, the door to the stairway was begging me, "hurry! Come! Save yourself!" I still don't know why we left the water in that truck. It was parked in the staff garage. I had to walk through the 'other side' of the building to get there. The nasty side. The side where all the evil gremlins of Galloway worked. There's a backstory behind those people's attitudes but it's far too political to get into right now.

>"Get'chur ass outta there, what are you doing!" an old scratchy voice said to me as I was walking into the threshold.

>*"Just headed to my car, sir. I'm with RUMB-"*

>He interrupted, "well, I don't much care, son. You see? My issue is that you'can't read."

My eyes slid to the far corners of their sockets. Back and forth like ping-pong.

>"See'that right'there?" he pointed to the door, "re-strict-ed-akk-sess. Eh? That means keep your ass out of there. And you're going in."

THE OTHER BLUE

In his defense, he was correct. It was a re-strict-ed-akk-sess sign plastered on the front of this door. I was definitely not headed to the garage. I had made an honest mistake but that old man knew nothing about those. At least, he acted like he didn't. Long story short, he calls for backup (other creepy old men with flashlights and extra batteries) and my journey for water (that poor, parched kid) turned into a crime scene. They took my ID and everything. It was difficult because they were old and decrepit. I will say they were in decent shape though. They were moving with a bounce that I haven't seen in old men since those viagra commercials that used to come on late.

Then a bigger, younger-looking, doctor (-esque) guy walked down the hall where they had me sitting. I'm pretty sure I was sober and I'm pretty sure it happened in slow motion. His white lab coat had a life of its own as it fluttered in the jet stream of his footsteps. Dude had to be at least 6'7, maybe 280 pounds. He had long black hair, too, like it was fresh out the shower. Just his hair, though. The rest of him could have used some sun and cocoa butter. He looked like he needed some water himself.

"Mr. Arrington," he sat next to me without looking at me. "You're with the radio station upstairs, correct?"

Just want to point out, again, that he still hasn't looked at me. We both were just sitting there staring at the wall, surrounded by those old guys with flashlights. It was quiet besides the walkie talkie chatter and random sounds echoing through the halls.

"Yes sir, we're doing Christmas giveaways and-"

"I know, I know. I popped up there," he responded. "Good work."

"Yes sir, it's one of my-"

He turned to me at an awkward angle, one that big dudes shouldn't try to do, saying, "listen. You just made a wrong turn, right? You're looking for -"

"Yes sir. The garage. Getting some water for a kid."

"Ok," he affirmed while awkwardly rising back to the ceiling.

I stood up too because I thought I had to.

"Come on, let's get you some water and get you back upstairs," he finished.

I followed the creepy doctor (-esque) guy but first, I had to look back down the hall. Those old security dudes were just staring at me. One of them opened a bottle of water. I thought he was just trying to be funny, you know? I don't know. I was just so creeped out, yeah. I was happy to get back upstairs.

***

"Why you ain't ever tell me that?" said Apple Pie. "Like, I never heard anything like that."

"Well, I ain't even mean to tell you that just now. It kind of just happened. I never really thought anything of it. Went back upstairs with the water, didn't even have to go to the truck. That big doctor guy brought a case up. Never said anything to me, just stopped and picked it up. Carried it and everything. Never really thought about that moment again. It was weird, though."

She replied, "weird as hell."

One thing I loved about Apple Pie is that she's one of those people who protected me my entire life. We walk this journey in hopes of meeting people like her. The ones we know will catch us when we fall. She gave me her word, her gorgeous word, that night. A promise to find those two detectives. She could tell I was spooked and at that point, I didn't even care to solve the case. I just wanted to stop seeing Jane Doe's face.

***

That's when I began writing PCW's initial report, the one that made the Times. I'm sure you've seen it before. That opening line, *cold and bare, Jane Doe stared at me and I heard her final heartbeat,* was written a few nights after that meeting with Apple Pie.

It was snowy (you probably guessed that) and Deja was in a rough stage of pregnancy. She was vomiting like a sick infant and would get these massive dizzy spells at night. I felt so bad for her. She couldn't even sleep some nights.

"Baby, do you still love me?" she asked with her hands wrapped around the toilet.

Her hair was in Canada. Her eyes were bathing in cranberry sauce. She burped.

"More and more each day, boo."

She closed her eyes on the bathroom floor, "what are you working on?"

The red lotus arose from the bathtub. She was kind of floating. Either that, or she was a lot taller than I remember. Water dripped from her naked body, hanging on to her piercings and bangles.

"Uh... I, uh...."

She responded, "why are you being like that about it?"

"Like...what?"

"Like...that. Weird. Like you're hiding something," she said, "is there something going on?"

My poor bride was as blue as the bottom of a dead woman's foot. She looked at me with piercing, but weak, eyes. It hurts to look back. I still hear the loud and violent dripping sound from the red lotus. I never looked at her though. Kept my focus on my bride.

"-Aus," Deja affirmed.

The daze, man. I always fall victim to the daze. It's happened a few times since you've been sitting here with me, honestly. I had to shake myself out of it when Deja called my name.

"You know, baby. Th-this…thing I'm working on. It's weird, you know? I feel like there's a story in it and I'm trying to piece it all together."

She looked away, "don't forget about our story."

It was definitive. Her tone, verbiage, energy; all of it was final.

"Baby… what? Never - what'chu mean?"

She replied, "just stay with me, tonight. Right here… please."

"I wasn't going anywhere in the first place. What are you talking about?"

"I know but just stay…Please," she said with an angel's kiss.

It was tough for so many reasons. I knew she wouldn't want me chasing a murder mystery let alone understand it. I'd done so much in my life by then. Loving me became quite the journey for her. A nauseating ride, you know? It was an interesting scene to think about while I watched her puke her pregnant guts out for hours. The red lotus slid back into the tub.

I had convinced her that it was best to get herself (and my twins) off the ground and into the bed. I baited her with the idea of watching the snowfall through the open blinds. It helped her fall asleep, you know. I loved it too. She didn't want to move at first. She probably would have stayed on that bathroom floor until it was time to give birth. We made our way to the bedroom and I tucked her in like my only piece of gold. The minute those eyes slid into the sandman's hands, I slid into the front room and began working on that report.

There was a story to be told and ImpactComm was going to tell it.

12 VELOUR

"Go to hell!" this homeless lady yelled at me in front of Galloway.

"Ma'am, I was just -"

"No! Y'go to hell! 'Don't want yo'fuckin' food, boy,'" she replied.

I had an extra sub because Deja didn't want hers. She was upstairs meeting with her delivery team. Well, it hadn't started yet. I dropped her at the door and went to park, you know the routine.

When I got into the maternity ward, I heard screaming. Man, it sounded like squirrels singing the National Anthem. Wait, no. It sounded more like the National Anthem singing squirrel. Even worse, it sounded like Deja. I ran from the stairway, knocking over papers at the nurse's station. They said something to me but whatever. I busted into the room with the screaming squirrel.

"Hey, you! Get the hell out of here!" a man hollered at me.

The doctors stared at me in their scrubs and the lady delivering the baby yelled, "get the hell out!" It certainly wasn't Deja. My eyebrows left the room before I did. I bumped into Deja while backing out of the room.

"Austin," she laughed, "I know you didn't think-"

*"Well, I don't know. I just heard a screaming lady...
Sounded like you and... I don't know."*

She smiled and rubbed my drooping face, "aw. You
do love your wife, huh?"

"More and more each day, " I replied.

She grabbed my hand, "come on."

The screaming squirrel became more and more
distant. Deja led me to the office where her (well, our)
doctors were meeting. 'Dr. Perfect' was there, too. After
shaking hands like we were buying a house, or something,
they instructed me to wait outside while they did some
pregnancy maintenance. You know, making sure everything is
working the way it's supposed to and discussing some of
Deja's more "private" concerns.

I was sitting in the hallway making music from all the
hospital sounds when a heavy-tailed force plopped down
next to me. I saw the lab coat dragging the ground before I
saw the person. Actually, it was the disgusting yellow nails at
the tips of those huge hands. It took me so long to find his
face. It was that scary ass doctor who got the water for me
last year (the year prior, I should say). What are the odds?

"Having a baby this time, huh?" he asked.

"Well... Yeah, man. That's my wife in there."

He replied with his mega-hand on my thigh, "good
for you, friend. That is really good."

I nodded with a smirk. It was uncomfortable seeing his hand swallow my thigh but it didn't feel sexual. Just felt like one of those "old sport" Gatsby type of things. By the time I had decided to say anything else, he had already disappeared with his lab coat floating in the wind.

"Mr. Arrington," a petite voice murmured, "you mind coming back for a minute?"

I heard Deja in the background, "no, he doesn't mind."

The room laughed a bit. It was sort of like a small studio audience welcoming me to the stage. They had her hooked up to all of these machines but assured me that nothing was wrong. She needed some fluids to help her system flow smoother. She also needed some pills too, I think it was a prescription strength supplement. I had to make sure she was taking those and this ginger-based drink. We also went over a few delivery options and prepared for the possibility of cesarean; you know, the usual "almost baby-time" stuff.

***

While I was standing in that room, still creeped out from the bighand Doctor (-esque) guy, all I could think about was the goddamn Gold Mic Ball. It happens once a year and they say the money was going to charity but who knows these days. I do have to be grateful for it because going to that godforsaken social catastrophe of epic proportions each year is part of what fueled my visions for Impact. It was an annual reminder that I was made for more. Radio wasn't as effortless as basketball but it was easier. It wasn't challenging.

I hated knowing that I could be at the top of the industry if I had just 'played the game'. I'm an athlete. Where I come from, you get to the top if you're the fucking best. Nothing less.

***

It was the week after and Deja had to stay home for obvious reasons. Which meant I was out in the field alone, dodging the bullets, laying on grenades, and playing hopscotch through minefields. The worst, man. If you ever get an invite from one of these types of events just burn it on site. Even if the goddamn fire causes your house to burn down, trust me it's worth it. Let it burn.

My suit was fly, though. It wasn't to impress anyone. I literally wore that green velour blazer because I felt good in it. Fashion for me was always about comfort. That's why I didn't wear that old gown today.

"Well, well," said this DJ named Scooby Major. "The big homie, Austin Arrington."

"Scoob, 'wassup man?"

He put his glass to his lips and his eyes smiled.

"Everything's everything, my man," he said after a gulp. "Headed out of town for a gig in London next week."

"That's awesome, man. Really dope."

"Yeah. Everything's paid for, my guy. Whew, them boys 'cross the pond be looking out," he continued.

"Yeah, man. They do. That's wassup."

"Right, right," he said, "so, 'wassup bro? You're done for real, huh?"

"Heh," I chuckled, *"-I mean… Man, it's time. My mind's been-"*

He interrupted, "wait, wait. Hold up- I'll be right back."

He started chasing one of the bigwigs who had just walked in. What an asshole. You know, I'll be honest about that moment. I was a little sad. My face was empty, but the inside was filled with emotion watching him walk away. It happened all the time. It was almost like I had some sort of repellant on me that prevented me from connecting with other people in this industry. I was a leader on the court, you remember? Of course you do. I'm a leader at home and even with all of those people outside of my circles who listened to me everyday in Echodale. They had an affinity for me. You remember how that field looked when I came crashing down with that blue'chute. It was just these people, the colleagues, that I had to "build" with. No one ever wanted to play with me.

***

The pretentious air was always hard for me to breathe. I blame my love of sports for that. It suffocates people on the court. Gold Mic was filled with it, though. So many stories of *Guess who I met last week* and, *Guess what job I just got.* Or my favorite, *We should link up.* I wouldn't call it a super power, but I could see through it all. Always have been able to.

"Not your kind of thing, huh?" said a sweet but domineering tone.

"[Gulp], I'm sorry?"

She continued, "this. Not really your thing, right?"

I laughed, *"what makes you say that?"*

"Well, you've been standing here for 15 minutes looking at everyone else. That dude with all those," she pointed to her face, "- Even when he was talking to you, I mean. It was all over your face. So, am I wrong?"

She took a devilish sip of her champagne (at least I think that's what it was). I saw the red lotus over her shoulder, sucking on an olive at a bar table. Then she ate it. Toothpick and all.

"The bigger question is, is this your thing? Sounds like you've been doing the same thing I've been doing."

"Debra Ray," she stuck out her perfect hand, "I work with your wife."

The red lotus smirked over Debbie's (is it too early for nicknames?) shoulder and then turned her golden back to me.

She continued, "Austin?"

"Oh, I…am….sorry about that. Thought I saw someone. Debra, nice to meet you. You… know me?"

"-And your wife," she nodded. "How is she?"

"She's doing much better, thanks for asking-"

"Oh, sure. Everybody's been asking," she continued.

My eyebrows responded before I did, *"I'm sure. She just had to go on maternity earlier than expected but she'll be back soon."*

It was silent for a few seconds. I heard the clinking of glasses off in the distance and the weightless chatter surrounding us.

"Hmph," she hurried the last swallow, "you see them over there? I bet you they're about to come over here."

"What?"

"Ten bucks. I bet you ten bucks. They've been all over the room. I bet they come over here and try to make a few funnies," she pleaded.

"Ok."

Sure enough they came over like those energy guys trying to sell solar power. I don't even remember where they were from or what they did. I just remember that annoying laugh that the woman had. She used it all the time. It's almost like she thought it was cute but everytime she laughed, it made me think of a dirt bike trying to start up.

"Or, them over there," Debbie said after the couple left us. "I won't take all your money so this one… This one, we'll do 5 bucks. I bet -"

"Wait, you know who that is right?"

Debbie looked confused, "should I?"

"Well, I don't know the lady but him? That's Cliff Jonah."

She affirmed, "ah, Cliff Jonah…"

"Yep."

"As in Cliff Jonah- " she looked up at me.

"Yes, you're boss," I laughed. *"How long have you been at the station again?"*

She laughed too. Debbie's a good sport but I really wanted to know. Deja had been talking about a new reporter coming into the studio soon so I figured it was her. Never thought she was playing games or anything.

Finally, she said, "ok, you've got me. I haven't even really started yet. Oh, but everybody is really asking about your wife. It's all online, you know?"

I laughed, *"so you haven't started yet then?"*

"Nope. Monday is the big day. But that Cliff guy is the one who- "

Mr. Jonah walked over, "- Deb. Great to see you here tonight."

He shook her hand and her smile shook his. It was a frantic smile. Think of a masked menace shaking hands with the police chief.

Then, "and Austin Arrington, always a pleasure, my friend. How's my girl?"

Ok, one: she's my girl and two, *"she's doing fine! Thanks for asking. She's at home resting right now. Her mother's in town, too. Everything's fine. Thanks for asking, sir."*

"Oh, most definitely. One of the best across all'our markets. We need to get you on there talking some hoops, too," he said like an egotistical frat boy. His hand patted my shoulder and everything. "Please, excuse me."

"So, he's the one who brought me from Baton Rouge," Debbie whispered to me as Cliff exited the scene. "At least, that was the rumor. Believe it or not, that was my first time meeting the guy."

"Good evening, ladies and gentlemen. Thank you for being a part of this year's Gold Mic," a sultry voice spoke from the podium. It was heavenly and angelic. Swallowed me into peace:

"- Each year, we get together and celebrate our industry, right here in Echodale -"

It felt like she was singing to me, you know? I looked up at the podium and my throat brewed a lump the size of a golf ball. There she was, Jane Doe, singing to me from that podium. The rest of the room disappeared, no other heartbeats. Just mine and Jane Doe's.

Mine was the only one I could vouch for, though.

13 APPLE PIE IS GOOD FOR THE SOUL

That night, I sat at my desk like a Pentagon secretary on 09/11. Thankfully, I was thinking fast at the Gold Mic and kept note of everything on my phone. She said her name was Sidney Garner. It was odd that my first time seeing-slash-hearing her was on stage at the ball. The people sure do annoy me but we are a small industry. Unfamiliar faces don't happen on this side of town.

***

"And you've never seen her before?" Apple Pie questioned from the corner of the room.

"Never. Like - ever, never, ever."

She leaned over the screen, "never?"

"- Never."

"And all of sudden she's the host of an annual event," she fell back into the shadows with her arms folded. "- I mean, you know everyone else…"

"Listen [redacted], I'm saying -"

"No, no, no. I'm not saying I don't believe you," she pleaded, walking back over to me. "I think I'm more like… thinking out loud. This is the same face you saw on'that table?"

I shook my head a few times. It was a desperate search for words and understanding.

> *"It certainly looked like it. Just like her."*

It got quiet.

> *"Wish I could see a better photo of this lady,"* I said as I continued typing away. *"She had...this thing... It was on her left ear."*

"Ok..." Apple Pie replied.

"...a hole. Think it's called an angel kiss."

She wanted to dig even more, "one of these," she pointed to her ear. "-Things... almost like a piercing."

I looked at her with a grin, *"precisely."*

It got quiet again.

She exclaimed, "nope. That'ain't it. "

"Hm?"

She got sassy and sarcastic with me, "it's not about the angel's thing. Unless you're trying to say that the dead girl is alive. Because that would be-"

"No, no... I mean, I'm just trying to put the pieces together."

"Well," she continued. "It sounds like you think Jane Doe was hosting the Gold Mics. That'ain't it."

Deja thumped the wall twice.

"Sorry!" we both exclaimed.

I threw my hands up away from the keyboard. I think I was getting a little sassy myself. I braided my arms and gave Apple Pie the keys because clearly I was driving us off of a cliff. Well, maybe not off it, but it wasn't the right direction. After all, one of us in the room was the professional and the other was just looking for a story. It's me, I'm the other.

"Listen," she began pacing the room, nearly kissing the floorboards. "We've got… We've got Jane Doe and a very much alive Sidney Garner-"

"Let's call her Sid."

She looked at me with a sarcastic smirk but a hint of disapproval, "ok, Sid… They look- well, are you sure she'looked like the dead girl?"

"*[Redacted], I dropped my drink*," I affirmed, "*shit spilled everywhere…*"

"Did she stop the show? Or, whatever y'all do in there?" she questioned.

"I mean, she had to. Yeah. It was loud… She made a joke, or something and went back to the service."

She scratched her chin where a beard would be, "ok, so she didn't notice you."

"No, I guess not."

"I wasn't asking, Austin," she said, "Just- I feel like you would know if she knew. You know?"

"Uh, yeah I think I do."

She began ravaging the room, "give me some paper, will'ya?"

"I could just send you this-"

"No," she affirmed. "-'best to keep everything old school. Just to be safe. That cloud stuff is what makes us all vulnerable…"

I forgot to mention how old-fashioned she was. But, she did have a point and again, only one of us was a professional. She wrote Sid's information down, everything we had discovered.

She shuffled, "I've got…to… get back home. Trey's probably starving. I'll call you tomorrow afternoon."

I didn't even have time to respond.

"Tell Deja I left some Apple Pie on the counter," she said as her voice fainted out of the apartment.

Deja's (even more fainted) voice replied through the wall, "thank you!"

But Apple Pie probably didn't hear it. She was long gone and halfway to Mexico in an instant.

***

I didn't get much sleep that night. I sat up with Deja (and her double-wide belly) in my arms, flipping through the sports channels. Perry's dominant year was continuing and that was all everyone was talking about.

"So, you guys are looking for someone," Deja murmured under my forearm.

Play dumb, play dumb!

"Wait, what? Who?"

"You and [redacted]. You know I could hear you. Y'all looking for someone," she replied. She never looked up but I certainly looked down. "Sid was hosting the Golden Mic this year, huh?"

"Wait, you know her? I've never seen her a day in my life."

"Yes, you have," she replied, turning to face me, "Sidney… Perry."

The TV blared: -Another big game from Armonti Perry, 47 points, 24 assists, and 13 rebounds; we'll check into Seattle coming up-
"No fucking way."

She turned back over, "she's been trying to get into TV and all of that. No'real talent, just… vibes."

I chuckled, *"hmph."*

***

We fell asleep an hour later. Stayed on the couch that night. Apple Pie called me in the middle of the next day. I saved my bit of information for the call and couldn't wait to hear hers. I used to try and act like I had it all together, you know that. If it was something to be dealt with, I wanted to be the one to do it. But this moment was different. It's weird because it wasn't necessarily difficult. The red lotus kept me company at every turn and just like her twirling me around Jane Doe's body in that cold room, she'd been pointing me in the right direction this whole time. I'm glad I learned to live with her. She's smiling at us, right now.

***

It sounded like a call center. Almost as if I had fallen asleep and woke up in the middle of a children's hospital telethon. We used to do those once a year, too. Usually just before the holidays. The Echodale Police Department has always been known for its high-tech and advanced appeal across the country but have you ever seen it? No really, have you?

I only visited Apple Pie in her office maybe twice. Both times I sat in that vestibule like a kid in Martin's (toy store back home) for the first time. All of those toys were just tinkering and twittering around me. She worked in the Blue Fifty brigade and that's all I'm going to say about that. It was always fun visiting her (those two times), though.

"Welp. You're in my house, now," she said while walking over to me, "it must be trouble."

I laughed. It was one of those big smiles I used to make during press runs after State games. Apple Pie did that to me. She was just a genuine, good person and you know what? She's a badass, too. I mean even when she walked over to me that day with her short sleeve black tee, combat pants, and boots, oh… and that beautiful CSX 9-millimeter on her waist. I mean, there's Bruce Willis (really cool) and then there's her (really fucking cool).

"No trouble, no trouble. But definitely some news."

Her eyebrows woke up, "oh, yes. About our… little situation, here."

"Here and there, sure."

She nodded her head before her eyes sailed off in the distance.

"Sure thing," she said while beginning to walk away, "just…hang out for a second for me."

The red lotus laid her soft and brown hand on my thigh, rubbing like she desired a fortune. I looked at her looking at me. Her pupils became gold. They were glowing, if you can imagine that. I kept staring and found freedom, a sudden richness of peace. We came closer as the seconds passed by. Like magnets in a 5th grade science class.

Apple Pie interrupted, "Austin? Come on." I looked around. It felt like both everyone and no one was looking at me. "Unless you want to grab some food."

"Naw, I just ate."

She continued, "Ok, cool. Come on back."

"You won't believe this shit," I said as I was taking my seat. *"So Dej-"*

"Whoa, whoa. Hold up for a second," she interrupted as she closed her office door. "Ok, now what?"

"Oh, my bad. So Deja heard us last night. She may have figured this whole thing out."

Apple Pie scratched that invisible beard, again.

"Sidney Garner?" I pleaded. *"Sidney…Perry."*

She stared at me with the blankest of stares. It was a little painful because I wanted her to understand it all. I wanted that 'aha' moment I had with Deja resting in my lap the night before.

"Sid Perry? You know…"

She looked empty, "should I?"

"Ok. That's Armonti Perry's first wife. You know me and-"

"Oh ok, ok," she said without a spark or concern. "-And you guys played together…"

"At state, yes. Actually fought, too."

"Wow. Good old-fashioned brothers, huh," she said sarcastically. It still wasn't that 'aha' moment, you know? I wanted a little more. "So, Sid Garner is Sid Perry?"

"With red hair and bigger boobs, yes."

She replied, "big-ger-boobs."

I nodded but she didn't see it.

She continued, "Well, I think Armonti has some answers then. Probably tough to get'em-"

"Already on it. I texted him this morning-"

She responded, "anything?"

"Nothing yet. They're in Houston tonight so, you know how that road life is."

"I don't but I have an idea," she said.

"*Ok, wassup?*" I said leaning in.

She laughed a little bit, "no, no. I have an idea about what 'road life' is like." She turned back to me, "so what we'll do is wait until we can get a response from your friend. I mean, maybe he can, you know… give us some information about his ex-whatever and we can use that somehow…"

"-*gotcha.*"

"It's tough, you know? Because the only reason we're even talking about Sid Gar-Perry, or whatever, is because you said she looks like your Jane Doe. That's it," she pleaded, walking back to the window. "I don't even know what we're really chasing, here. You know?"

I knew what had to happen next. So do you.

"*Ugh,*" I let out, "*well… You've just gotta see her.*"

She drooled, "I knew you were going to say that.

14 BACK IN CHILL

The bell at the front desk sounded young and spunky. That same old lady with the scruffy voice waddled into the gate. Her glasses were miles thick and were the only thing keeping her company behind the desk. She stared at me and Apple Pie without saying a word, chewing a goddamn piece of gum in surround-fucking-sound. We literally stood there staring at each other before Apple Pie spoke.

"Um, yes, hi," she said. "So I'm detective [redacted] and we're investigating a case involving a Doe."

The old lady smacked the gum even harder, somehow.

Apple Pie continued with wide eyes, "ok. This-gentle-man-here... was - called - down - to - ID - a bo -dy," she emphasized poetically. "I - am - a - detec - tive - on - the - case - and - I - want - to - see - it - too."

She pulled out her badge just as soon as she finished that last word.

The old lady smacked harder. Damn her. I'm getting upset about it again. She cut those big eyes at me and looked me up and down as if I owed her money.

"Name?" her scratchy voice asked.

"Yes... Um, my name is Austin. Austin Arrington."

I don't know why there was a standoff between us. Our eyes were just fighting, man. Then she finally told us to have a seat and we spent the next few moments watching bodies roll in and out. One body had an arm pop up through its body bag. Scared the hell out of me. Death care is lucrative and never ending. Shout out to the funeral homes. Let me hold something.

"Arrington," the scratchy voice purred.

"Yes?"

The old lady didn't respond. She just stared at me through the top of her glasses chewing that damn gum. You know, I stopped chewing gum around that time, too. I think it was her fault. My experience with this lady and her pet-gum made me hate the entire industry.

"We don't have a record of you'here, son," she scratched.

"That's... Impossible. I wa-"

"- what? Just here?" she interrupted. "You weren't... Because if you were, then your name would be right here."

I was confused. Slightly embarrassed, too. I turned to Apple Pie who was leaning against the wall in the corner and she mouthed, *you good?* I put up that one finger that says, *I'm not good but give me a minute and I will be.*

"Son," the old lady scratched once more, "is there anything else I can do for you?"

Her gum kept talking. Actually, it was more like rapping.

> *"Listen, ma'am. There must be some sort of... mistake. You see, I was just here. I remember you..... And-and... last time there was another lady here. They brought me back to identify a body,"* I pointed to the eerie hallway (that I'll never forget). *"It was a doct-"*

Her gum stopped rapping and said, *shut the fuck up.* The old lady just stared. I think she fell asleep with her eyes open. Her face twisted like she was standing next to the most active landfill in the city. I tapped the desk. The corners of my mouth admitted defeat.

"What's going on?" Apple Pie questioned as I walked over.

"Well... I don't exactly know how to say this," I cautioned like a trapeze artist walking a piece of hair. *"She says that she has no record of me here."*

Apple Pie came off the wall, "what?"

"I know. But- You have to believe me. I was right there just a few days ago-"

The old lady scratched loudly, "-you two keep it down, I'm trying to watch my staw'ies!"

My phone was buzzing in my pocket and it felt kind of good but I'll never admit that to anyone else. I reached for it but Apple Pie's voice froze me.

"That one was for me," she affirmed.

I slid my hand out of my pocket; slow and steady. Didn't want to startle my enraged friend. Her vanilla face had turned strawberry and the steam coming from her ears smelled like a milkshake.

She led, "come on," and marched to the counter, "hi. It's me again. Detective [redacted]. He says he was here a few days ago to ID a body. You say he wasn't." She pulled out her badge, "this says that you have to show me the security footage and I can get my answers and go on about my day."

It was another standoff between us and the gum. I started to think the old lady was just a proxy and her body was being controlled by evil gum from another galaxy.

"They're broken," the old lady scratched in the most uninterested tone known to man.

I shouted, "*Lattisaw and MeDerra! You... have to remember those two. They met me here and asked me about the lady... Lattisaw and-*"

"-MeDerra," Apple Pie continued. "They were here too. That ring a bell?"

***

It didn't.

Within minutes, we were back on the streets of Echodale watching ambulances drop off more bodies. Not going to lie, I thought about just waiting until that old geezer got off work and jumping her. I would never say that publicly, though. She just put us both in a bad mood and we were sitting there trying to gather ourselves again.

"You go home, I'll get in there," she affirmed. "Be by the phone, Austin. I call, you pick up."

The friendly version of Apple Pie had run its course and she was now in commando-mode. Or, more like Bond, or Sherlock. This is how she ended up so decorated today. One hell of a service woman and she really gave me her all, you know? A friend and protector.

***

A few hours later, I was getting out of the shower when Armonti finally texted me back. I told him that we needed to speak over the phone. He called but at the same time, a dainty-knock tapped on our apartment door.

"Deja, Deja!" the voice said.

The voice. I knew only one person who had it. Only one person had that feeling that made us feel as warm as the sands of Paradise.

"Jazzy!" Deja yelled from the couch. She wanted to get up but the double-wide belly didn't. "Austin, get the door! Get it!"

THE OTHER BLUE

"But, babe… I'm naked."

She replied, "oh, it's just Jasmine, boy." Dragging her head above the back of the couch, "you'got a towel! Just open the door."

So, I did and that damn cat from next door scurried in first. It was the brown one that never looked like it wanted to be alive. I reached down to grab it so quick, I was quite proud of myself. The red lotus was, too. I heard her clapping while she swung her legs on the counter-top.

Jasmine was still as pretty as Paradise. As you can imagine, she and Deja had grown quite fond of each other since the honeymoon. Tragedy will do that to you. I was so happy to see her.

"Don't get up, don't get up," Jasmine said as she glided into our apartment.

I threw the brown cat back into the hallway and shut the door quick enough to keep it out forever. Quicker than whatever you're imagining right now.

"Ohhhhhhhhh!" Jasmine said as she hugged her friend as tight as a fresh braid.

"I guess I'll just go get dressed," I said down the hall.

The ladies giggled like schoolyard girls. I tried to call Perry back but of course, I got no answer. I was standing there in my boxers, the blue ones that made me feel like a man. The red lotus stared at me from the corner. Her eyes had a way of talking. I didn't even have to see them. She had a worry on her heart that hovered in the middle of the room like dark clouds of a hurricane.

"Babe," Deja whispered from the bedroom door. "You ok?" She was holding that belly like the gold that it was.

I turned, *"oh yes. I'll be out in a minute. Jus'trying to get with Armonti."*

"Isn't he on the road?" She asked.

My head responded before I did.

"Yeah, he is. I'll be out in a second."

***

I never understood my fascination with taking showers. Even late at night, I would refresh in the shower and throw on new clothes. I'd change outfits twice, maybe 3 times a day. I didn't get it. My therapist thinks it's nervous energy trying to find its way out of my system.

"Well, if it isn't Mr. Arrington," Jasmine lulled me into the front room.

"Jazz, you made it. Welcome to 'Merica."

"Agh," Deja stuck her tongue out. "This place is a beautiful disaster.

Jasmine smiled, "so poetic, my love." It was her accent that always drew me in. A magnetic tone. "Well, let's hope I don't see any of that... - stuff."

"Would you like a drink?"

"Oh, yes, yes. Si," she perked up. "What's over there?"

"Well, we've got some Pearson... Uh-," I had to get up to go look. *"- That sweet whiskey stuff... Some Calumet. A couple options."*

She melted into Deja's eyes and rubbed her belly. "I don't know, I hate options.... Just- just give me the sweet stuff, eh."

"Sweet stuff coming up."

My phone started ringing as I was bouncing around the kitchen. It only rang a few seconds before I choked it. I was pouring the drink and it rang again. I was quicker on the draw that time.

"Um, so, Austin," Jasmine sang. "-put me on with one of your friends." The ladies giggled louder than lovers at the fair.
"Eh, what?" I chuckled nervously.

Half of that nervous energy was me trying to focus on that drink. Damn thing kept trying to escape the cup.

"Nah, don't put that pressure on me," I said as I searched for a rag.

"-Nuh,uh, Austin, what'chu mean? Jazz would be perfect for Dee," Deja pleaded.

"Yeah, she would. I mean, I know that much. But, I'm saying - them others? You know some of them are a little-"

She cut her eyes at Jasmine who was painted with the brightest of smiles. "- yeah, a little - eh," my bride replied.

My phone started ringing again. It was silent this time. I didn't recognize the number and you know how bill collectors can be. I didn't want to answer it and get drawn into one of those painful interrogations over a few hundred dollars. Looking back, yeah, it seems unusual that a bill collector would call persistently like that. We're talking 5 or 6 calls within a ten minute window. My mind was stuck on making it all make sense but my face was stuck on happiness. A few brain cells were managing the conversation of the room and a few more were managing the bar (I know it wasn't a real bar, don't rub it in).

"So don't be shy, Jazzy," I said as I handed her the drink, *"you'got them eyes on someone, don't you?"*

They giggled and curled up even more. It reminded me of growing up with my two cousins, Lisa and Jordan, swooning over the season's heartthrob. They were two pretty peas in a pod and every family function became an interrogation of their dating life. It was cute because they were so sweet and shy. The giggling was mostly nerves but they loved the attention. I miss them.

"Jazz…" Deja giggled with her wobbling belly. "I showed her that picture from the reunion," her eyebrows blushed at me.

"Oh, you do have your eyes on someone, huh?"

"No, no. You two calm'a down," she smiled. "I don't have the time for anything like that-"

My phone started ringing again, dragging my smile down. Deja saw me look at it and put it away. I shook my head so she knew not to ask. Everything was fine. At least, I hoped so. Just a bill collector who really wanted their money.

"Derry's here!" Jasmine said. She sprung up as if Derry was her father returning home from war. "Oh, I haven't seen him in so long."

Deja nodded at me as if to say *yeah, I invited Derry too.* I didn't have an issue with the company, or anything. When you've got a baby on the way you know your house can randomly become a rec center. Family from thousands of miles away and friends from around the corner, all meeting in your living room (drinking your sweet stuff), hoping to bring good vibes to your home. What's there to complain about? I mean, seriously. Who would complain about such a thing?

***

A few moments passed and there he was walking into my apartment. We already knew he was coming (thanks to Jazz's announcement) so I met him at the door. I was standing there watching him get off the elevator. He was just as excited to see Jasmine, if not more. He was bubbling with an explorer's glow. She flew into his arms and he twirled her in the sky; you may have thought they were father and daughter.

"Ow, shit, Derry," Jasmine said (it was even funnier with her accent).

He laughed and almost dropped her, "-are'you alright?"

"I don't know, I mean... 'May have to call my lawyer, yeah?" Jasmine laughed. "- Yeah?"

"Now, now," Derry leaned in as she held her hand on her head. "You've only been here for a few seconds and you already want my money."

She laughed with shy shoulders and curled into Derry's arms, "mmhm."

I hurried them back into the apartment before one of those damned cats got any bright ideas. We sat around the front room like the family that we were. Laughter filled the air like smoke at a pool hall.

"- Yeah, how is Braun?" Deja asked Jasmine who responded with her body language before her tongue.

Then she replied, "eh, well…The last few days have been 'ok'. But, it's been - a rough road since you guys left. Paradise has…. Changed."

"Wow," Deja replied.

Then I chimed in, *"well, I mean. What's been going on? He seemed pretty put together…"*

Derry finally began undoing his brown leather coat and unplugging his perfect hands from his gloves.

"Lefthand, I think it was me. 'Think I gave him more than what he could handle," he sighed.

"It's that bad?"

Derry and Jasmine shared a moment before he turned to me, "it is." He continued, "-too much, too quick."

"Are'you 'gonna do anything about it?"

He responded, "Well, we may not have a choice. At this point…"

"Ok, no," Jasmine spoke into the somber air. "We're supposed to be laughing and celebrating this right here…" She rubbed Deja's belly (who must've enjoyed it a little bit - you should have seen her face).

"Yeah, I know. We'ain't know asking about Braun was 'gonna be like that."

Derry responded like a disappointed father, "we didn't either."

It was sad and definitive. I felt the door slam on that particular conversation but I knew that it would come back up. His eyes told me so and they begged me to ask him later. I nodded at the unspoken request as my phone kept vibrating in my pocket.

"Derry," Jasmine began. "Have you got yourself a'home?"

"He's got two," Deja responded.

Jasmine got excited. I mean, she damn near fell out of her chair. The drink was strong, though. Maybe that had something to do with it. The front door camera got me and Deja's attention. Apple Pie was just about to ring the doorbell, looking as frantic as an addict on a dealer's steps.

Deja pushed, "you'wanna get that?"

"Definitely, definitely."

I felt the curious eyes of the room follow me to the door. They continued conversation but it was light enough to manage both the chatter and the mysterious visitor. The red lotus was standing at attention when I walked past the kitchen threshold on the way to the front door. She startled me but her beauty was still peaceful. I opened the door.

"Can we talk for a second?" Apple Pie requested.

We greeted each other with that awkward *hey*. I'm sure she heard the voices in the room so she probably didn't want to interrupt. The fact that she did kind of told me that she had to.

"Hell yeah, come on in."

She stepped in with confidence, "-hey!"

Everyone yelled back, "hey!"

"This is [redacted]," I introduced the room. "[redacted], these are our friends all the way from Italy."

"Italy? Wow. Well, welcome to Echodale!" said an excited Apple Pie.

Derry and Jasmine looked at each other and then Derry looked at me. Deja looked at Apple Pie and then Apple Pie looked at me. Derry bounced his eyes between the two of us, standing over the front room like we had somewhere to be. He then dropped his eyes to Deja who then turned and looked at me.

"Ok, then. Give us just a minute. She wants to go over something," I said, *"babe, just a minute."*

She held her stomach in sarcasm, "yeah, I'm not going anywhere."

The conversation continued in the front room as we walked down the hall, into the office. I closed the door gently enough to not draw attention. You've got to be careful with these things. One wrong move and the pregnant one will have your head on a platter and served at the feast of bad husbandry. They swear it's not a thing but the older I get, the more guys I know who were on the menu. Sad story. They disappear and they're gone forever, kid.

"Jesus [redacted], what's going on?"

She ignored my whisper and chose a slightly higher volume, "well, I tried to call you. Texted you too."

"My phone's been going dumb all night. Some weird number," I pulled out my phone. *"Oh, wait. That was you that called the last time."*

Her eyes swelled and her head bobbled. If *'I told you so'* had a look, imagine that.

"Yeah?" she questioned. "Listen, can you get away tonight?"

"No... but, what time you tryna'meet?"

She smiled, "- well. Hm. It just has to be before morning. But tonight, though."

"What's going on?"

She held up a key fob, "we're getting into the morgue and you're 'gonna show me our Jane Doe."

I dropped my head. Listen, I'm a natural athlete and businessman. The police field and all that other edgy shit was not my calling. Part of me knew I should have never gone to Apple Pie and just let the whole thing blow over. She's one of those people that get turned on by things like this. But I looked at those wandering eyes and those eyelashes waving me over. I knew it was going to be a long night.

"I'll run home first and then I'll park around back until you're ready," she affirmed.

I never got a chance to reply actually. She left the room like someone was writing her a parking ticket. I returned back to the front room with a heavy night ahead. I tried to ignore it all and enjoy the company. I shouldn't say "try" because I did. It ended up being a decent night with people that we love.

***

We waved our magic wand into the cold and quiet morgue. The door's creaking echoed into the waiting room. Thank God that old lady wasn't there. The gate was down at the receptionist's desk and the lights were dim. The TV was still on, though. It was playing weird infomercials with that guy with the box haircut.

"Why are you tiptoeing?" Apple Pie asked me. She didn't hold back with her sarcastic grin.

"I thought that's what we were supposed to do…"

She laughed, "no, we're supposed to be here, remember? We have a key."

That same look you're making, I did the exact same thing. Don't ask because I didn't. I just un-crouched my back and walked with the detective through the morgue.

"Hey!" a voice snuck over our shoulders. "-say, wait there."

Apple Pie flashed her badge, "Detective [redacted], Echodale PD. We-"

"Oh, sorry ma'am. I, uh, didn't know," the man said.

"It's fine. You were supposed to ask. Thank you for doing that," Apple Pie exclaimed with a hint of charm. "We're here on a case. A doe. Eh, what's your name?"

He replied under Apple Pie's spell (that actually sounds good), "Thomas. Thomas Getchian."

"Ok, Thomas. If you don't mind, I may can use some'a that help of yours. You seem like quite the guy," she continued.

He smiled, "aw, well. You'know… I do try. I'll be here."

"Great. We'll be right back, then. Your drawers are-" she began.

"-hm! My drawers?" he asked.

"Yes. Your cold drawers. The bodies," she replied.

He calmed himself, "oh, yeah. Sure. They're everything past that set of double doors."

His keys sang as he pointed down the hall. The green light from the exit signs above pretended to light the way. Only one of us was concerned about the dark. This is what makes her one of the best in the business, though. Nothing scared her. She always had a tongue that could part seas and lead revolutions. I think it really just speaks to how sharp of a mind she is.

We stood just beyond the doorway and stared into the room of cold gurneys and white sheets with humps in them. It was only six but that was six too many, for me. I just couldn't show any fear. Not 'gonna lie about it. I think I was fighting to be tough because of the whole 'gender-norm' conversation that we all avoid.

"All I need you to do is walk with me as I pull back the sheets. That's it. It'doesn't even have to be long- nothing crazy or drawn out. Nothing like that," she pleaded. "I just need to see the face then see Sid's. Cool?"

"Cool. (literally)"

We began around the room. I quickly ruled out the first two because they were significantly bigger than I could Imagine my Jane Doe's body being. Apple Pie still lifted the sheet. I waved them off.

"Ok, what about this one?" she said from the corner of the room.

It was a blonde-haired, middle-aged woman with freckles. They were still very much alive on her very cold face. I forced myself to lean in just a little closer. It looked like she was smiling.

"-Nope. But doesn't it look like she's... like she's smiling, or something?"

Apple Pie smiled, herself. Just a little bit though. Actually, it was more like a *'really?'* type of look. She dropped the sheet and walked over to the next gurney.

"This can't be it," she said as she lifted the sheet back. "Pretty sure this is a guy, right?"

"I don't know, but it's not who we're looking for-"

She nodded her head. We were down to the final body and suspense was killing me (no pun intended). This last one had to be her. I honestly didn't know how I would react when I saw her face again. I felt like I knew all about her and heard her story from the moment I saw her. The demons that danced around her. They were dancing for me too. I just didn't know what I would do.

"Let's see if this is it. If not, then… I don't know," Apple Pie said as she held the sheet in her hand. "Oh, damn."

"What?"

"Well," she said, "I know this ain't it."

It was an asian woman. She was the most peaceful of the bunch. I wish they had biographies or something because I would have loved to know her story. Her last few seconds on earth had to have been comforting.

"So… So, now what?"

She leaned up against the tray table resting beside our peaceful asian. The toes of her combat boots tangled across her ankles and her arms rested on her breast, braided like pretzels.

"Well, I don't fucking know," she said. "You've got to show me a face, Austin. I just don't… I just don't know anymore."

"What? You don't believe me?"

She stood up with a frustrated chest, " it's not that, bro. Not at all. It's just… this is somebody else's case. Kind of. And… For me to walk into it, it's like. It has to be something. I believe you… Like, I'm not saying you're lying but I've got to know what we're working with, here…Wait-"

She hopped around the room checking the drawers like a mad-woman. She opened each one. You know, like a K-9 sniffing out a drug mule at the border. She went through every drawer without a hint of fear and only found 3 bodies; 3 of which weren't Jane Doe.

"Fuck me, man," she said as she fell up against a tagless drawer.

Footsteps arrived at the swinging double doors, "Oh yeah? Is that a firm request? Or… Is that more like a demand? Either way, I'm all in. No pun intended, of course."

I knew that voice.

15 Back in Chill II

It was one of those moments that startled you so much that you didn't even jump. It's like, in those situations, we choose to just deal with whatever is coming. As if the last grain of sand has cleared the hourglass. We didn't have anywhere to go, it's true.

"Who the hell are you talking to like that?" Apple Pie flexed into heroic posture. "-eh?"

"Whoa, whoa," the voice responded, walking into the scarce light of the room. "Let's… let's just, bring it down a notch. Only kidding, only kidding."

It was Lattisaw. His coat was so long that I feel like it needs a name, too. We'll call his coat Jerome. Of course Mederra was tailing the rear, clinging on to Jerome's tail like an attention-whore toddler. They had on the same wing-tipped shoes but only one wore them confidently.

"Jesus, Austin. Where'd you find this one?" Lattisaw continued. "This'ain't Deja."

I was silent.

Apple Pie sliced, "Austin?"

"No, this is my friend [redacted]. [redacted], this is uh, well, these are two detectives I met a few weeks back. Lattisaw and MeDerra. I believe you guys are with the FBI, correct?"

Lattisaw continued to smile in the light, "sure. A little bit of this… -little that. Everything, everywhere these days."

Apple Pie looked at me and our eyes were talking. They were sitting at a conference room table at the Pentagon discussing what the hell was going on. Hers remained stoic but what else would you expect? She's everything that I've advertised and some. Trust me on that.

He danced, "-so, what brings you guys to the Gallo-way-Gen-er-al Morgue? Huh, looking for a friend?"

"Well, I think I uh, think I got a lead on that case and…Needed to come down to see her face again."

He replied, "Ohp! Wait a minute now, kid. What the hell are you talking about?" His hands brushed 'Jerome' aside to brandish his gun. "I've never seen you before. T'hell you talking?"

"What?" Apple Pie mumbled.

Her eyes didn't though. It was weird and I'm really trying to explain it. I stood there, dumbfounded with a mind that was scrambling like an overworked diner.

"I-UH-"

Apple Pie reached for her waist, "Austin, what the hell is this?"

"Ah, so either your 'friend' is more than...a friend," Lattisaw said while descending on Apple Pie. "Or... Well, she's illegally carrying a firearm onto government property... And you know the penalty for that, don't you.... Detective?"

By the time he finished his monologue, he was hovering over Apple Pie's shoulder with his hand on his gun.

It got unusually silent before Lattisaw shouted, "Austin Arrington! It's a pleasure to meet you."

His tongue was dancing more than when we first met.

"What? Lattisaw, we've-"

He replied, "uh uh, I don't think we've ever met."

He walked over to extend his hand and I shook it. Truthfully, I felt that I didn't have much of an option. I guess I didn't really shake his hand but my reflexes did. It was slow and calculated; a bit nervous, if I'm being honest.

"You guys looking for this?" MeDerra yelled from the doorway, looking as dumb as the handles on it.

Lattisaw replied, "MeDerra!"

Finally, he held up an urn. It was a glossless silver, as sad as you can imagine. If I opened it, I feel like I would have heard Ave' Maria playing on a loop.

THE OTHER BLUE

"We weren't looking for anything."

Lattisaw crept up to me and engaged in this standoff, of sorts. His eyes were wasting so much energy but mine were actually confident. I saw her standing over his shoulder. The red lotus. Standing there smoking a cigarette, blowing Os like she was in a music video. I knew everything was going to be fine.

He whispered with a smoking tongue, "now get the hell out of here before I decide to do my job."

His gun cocked. I thought it woke our (smiling) dead asian. It certainly woke Apple Pie whose face was painted with all sorts of aggression. She was like the neighborhood Pitbull who is always primed to break the leash. Unfortunately, I had to step in and make sure that didn't happen. I was going to be a father for the first time and I wanted to make sure that day came for me. I also wanted Apple Pie to get back home to Jacob.

"[Redacted], let's get you home."

She didn't fuss or fight; didn't say a word. Our 6 new friends watched us leave and the smiling dead asian giggled us out.

16 04:17 AM

"You should have let me kill them," Apple Pie exclaimed. "I'm EPD. You were there... You've been to my precinct. You- you..." she pulled out her badge, "-you see this. Don't you think we would recognize each other?"

"Yeah. That's why I said FBI back there. He never said anything about that. I made it up and he-"

She looked over at me while trying to manage the road. In fact, she looked over twice. I could see the lightbulb getting some power above her head.

"Well," she said looking back at the road, "you still should have let me kill them. Boff'em."

"[Redacted]!"

We swerved into the service lane around an oncoming semi. Scary as hell, man. It happened so quickly. Shook us both. Our breaths raced each other as we maneuvered back onto the road.

"You ok?"

She replied, "I'm fine."

***

Did you know that our ceiling fan spun at approximately 4 MPH? Of course you didn't, you've never been to that apartment. What am I saying? I knew that, though, because I watched that damn fan all night that night. Deja and her belly were sleeping peacefully in my left arm and all I could do was count the number of times that fan swung. It never put me to sleep but it did put me in a daze. I saw myself in the widest of fields with miles and miles of dandelions. I was shirtless chasing Jane Doe and she was dressed in a white skirt-set with a small floral pattern across the chest. She kept turning around, giggling, begging me to keep chasing her. I kept running. I closed my eyes and opened them again. That's when I saw the red lotus standing up against the far wall of the bedroom with her head leaned back. Pain was in her eyes. I'd never seen her like that before.

I did something bad a week later. Not villainous but, I just felt weird.

***

"Hey man. Mr. Seattle!"

Perry replied off camera, "who me? Man, I'm just trying to do something. You know how it is."

I nodded.

He said, "hello?"

"-yessir! My bad, I was over here nodding. But yeah, we know how you steppin' this season. How's the uh, the ankle?"

He replied, "man. This damned thing just… Always trying to hold me back, bro. Hopefully, I'll be back out there against Cleveland."

"I hope so, too."

He replied coming back into the screen, "you know we'll be out there next week."

"Naw, I lost track of time, bro. Things'been a little hectic over this way."

"Oh yeah," he stared into the camera. I could feel his tone shift; still warm and lighthearted but concerned. "You good?"

"Yeah, man. We're good, we're good. Just the pre-baby life and-" I stopped and looked up at Apple Pie, sitting in the shadows like the FBI during a phone tap. *"-just a project that's been killing me."*

He replied with stern eyes, "ah, damn. Well honestly, bro. I'm just happy you'doing your thing, you know? But if you need something just let me know. 'Hope we can link next week."

"Thanks, man. I hope so, too."

There he was floating away from the screen, again. He was all over his lavish backdrop.

"Damn, I uh- I feel 'kinda bad, now," he sunk.

"Why, bro? Wassup?"

He replied, "nah because I was hitting you up about the documentary. -but I mean, whenever you got time-" He swam back to the camera and continued, "-whenever you got time, we can pick it back up."

"Nah, it's cool. It's cool...I tell you what, we'll sit down and get things squared away next week when you get here. If you can get some time away."

"Ok, cool," he replied, "no doubt. I'll just fly back like Wednesday morning, or something. Think we actually have the rest of the week off."

I glanced at Apple Pie's impatient eyes.

"Bet, bro," I continued. *"-You get my text last week, bro?"*

His entire demeanor changed.

He was increasingly confident in his tone, "-ah, yeah. I hit you right back. We'was scrimmaging when you text me. You good?"

"Ah, ok...ok. Yeah, I'm good, I just needed your help with something."

"Shoot," he replied.

"Ok. I was just 'gonna ask... You talked to Sid, lately?"

His face scrunched like an antique accordion from Dallas.

He dipped, "Sid...Garner? My ex-wife?"

You should have seen the air leave the room. Even Apple Pie could feel how hard the question hit. An atom bomb. The cloud hovered like a deep fart of an obese king.

"I know, man. But, yeah. Sid Garner."

"Hell nah," he brushed. "Hell to the nah. Bro, between you and me, man. Man... I hoped she dropped dead the minute we got 'outta that courtroom."

We laughed but Apple Pie didn't. Actually, I don't think I was naturally laughing, either. It was more like a nervous giggle.

"Nah, man. Forreal," he continued. "That girl wiped me clean. I mean, well, not clean. I'm still good but still. She'wild, yo."

I lightened the mood with a true lie, *"-bro, I forgot y'all was a thing."*

"Yeah, well I didn't. That girl living good," he shrugged. "-Why'you ask about that bitch?"

That was harsh. I mean, the 'b-word' has always been the sharpest explicative in the shed to me but he delivered it with some extra 'umph'. It was a haymaker in an Ali fight. His tongue's best punch. But, you guessed it; just a nervous giggle from me.

"-well, she was here a few weeks back. She hosted the Gold Mics and I was trying to get in touch with her about it but I'ain't realize she was who she is until Deja reminded me. I was like, 'damn'," I leaned back.

"Man, that bitch is hell," he affirmed, "but you'trying to work with her? She'don't do shit."

"Well, I just-"

"Like," he interrupted, "why was she even hosting that? What?"

"I don't know. No offense but she was 'kinda trash, too."

He affirmed, "Oh, you not offending me. I couldn't care less. But yeah, I'll just- I don't know, I'll just hit her sister and give her your number."

Lightbulb.

"Oh, she's got a sister? In Echodale? Or.."

He replied, "nah. She's here. They'both from Seattle. I'll give her sister your number and she can pass it to Sidney. I just can't deal with that girl, man."

"My dog. Thanks, man."

The rest of the conversation was a trip down memory lane. It was completely random, too. It actually felt good to sit there and reminisce with Armonti. I was proud of him. Apple Pie probably didn't hear a single word of our storytime because she was hard at work. I didn't know she was working until later but she was tying up the loose ends of this mystery and connected the dots of Perry's words. I said it before and I'll say it a million times over, Apple Pie is worth every penny. Both the dessert and the detective.

***

Project Cold Wednesday had gotten about 10 pages long. I wanted to share it with Deja so bad but I always thought it would scare the hell out of her. I wish I did because when she found out, it really wasn't that big of a deal. Plus, she had her ear to our (thin) walls everytime Apple Pie came over. Me and Sid had been texting back and forth.

We'd made plans to connect in Echodale the same week that Armonti was supposed to be in town. Trust me, I made sure that it was a different day. I know you probably would love to hear about that rendezvous going wrong but you do understand that I just couldn't risk that. It was only going to be me and her. Apple Pie wanted to take things to another level and slide a wire down my black tee for the meeting but I just couldn't do that. Not this time. Maybe another.

That next week wound up being a week from hell.

17 Wow, it's Monday

Monday arrived and my coffee tasted like pizza. Stiff pepperoni and a strong onion-based sauce. That's when I realized that it was pizza. Cold pizza and a piping hot brew. It was a weird combination but I never said I was sane. In fact, I cannot guarantee my sanity from this point on. You're just going to have to bear with me.

The thing was, I had been so flustered with life that I began dipping my pizza into my coffee. It dripped onto my cheap black desk and it was so low budget, I feared the coffee would burn through it. I knew I'd be a jerk for asking my pregnant wife to help with the clean up so I got to scrubbing like poor little Annie, singing her song.

Pah-kow, pah-kow. I heard gunshots outside of the window.

"Deja!"

She hollered (with an annoyed tongue), "WHAT!"

Ok, clearly she's fine, I thought. She didn't even hear them. I got up to go peak and *pah-kow*, another shot rang off just as I reached the windowpane.

Would you believe that my damn passenger window was shattered? I mean, completely shattered. It was tinted and I could see the window had completely fallen apart but was resting in the adhesive; me and the window both wanted to cry. You know I'm a car guy. It had three gunshot wounds and there wasn't a trigger-man (or woman) in sight.

"No, no, no, no," I ran into the front room.

She responded, "hon-... Baby! What's wrong?"

"You didn't hear that shit?"

Her eyes searched the room for words, "-hear what?"

"Baby... Somebody just shot my window. You didn't hear that?"

"Shot your window?" she parrotted, "Like- gunsh-"

"Yes. Somebody literally just shot my window. The passenger side... It's.... It's three bullet holes in my shit right now!"

I was so frustrated. You've been living long enough to understand my colorful language. I'm sure you've been at that point in life where things just seem to pile up on each other. You may make it through the minefield but end up having to dodge bullets on the other side. Then you have to lay on a few grenades. That's how it felt and truthfully, I wanted to cry. Not only was I trying to be a man, I was trying to understand what that meant. At that time, I felt like it meant that I needed to run outside and see what the hell was going on. Deja responded to my last few words but I couldn't tell you what she was talking about. You can imagine that she was ready to waddle down those steps and into the cold. I told her to keep writing and let me handle it.

I think that if you sing the "ABC's" song one time all the way through, that's how long it took me to get to the main floor. I ran past the mailbox corridor and into the first set of double doors leading to the parking lot where my lovely chariot was parked. I didn't go through the second set because I realized that the shooter could still be out there. I had kids that I wanted to meet, you know?

This part is our secret, Deja never knew it. I stopped at the second set of doors and leaned up against the cold glass to cry. I let it all out right there. There wasn't anyone around; no pregnant wife to be strong for, no weird (maybe) detectives, no actual (super strong) detectives, no mega-successful ball players to remind me of my failure (that I try to pretend didn't happen), and no foreigners that I had to pretend I always knew the answers for. It was just me and that cold glass. It spoke the language of my heart.

After the tears slowed themselves I decided to call EPD. Looking back, maybe I should have called Apple Pie but I didn't want to bother her, for whatever reason. I kind of didn't want to see her. It was the weird point of seeing someone too much, sometimes you just need a break. I was immature, though.

The timid lady slid, "Echodale Police, what's the address of your emergency?"

"1605 Genesee, Apartment 16 but the parking lot."

She replied, "-O…K. Thank you and what's the emergency?"

"Gunshots. Ther- there are three of them in my passenger window. No one's around…. I was in my office and heard them, looked down and well, my car is shot up, ma'am."

She replied, "- OK....dispatch shots fired, Lafayette Towers, all nearby officers respond. Shots fired, Lafayette Towers - and sir, has anyone been shot?"

"No. No one is even... It doesn't look like anyone is out here. We were upstairs when it happened."

I didn't go back upstairs. I needed more time with that cold glass. After maybe the first two tracks of your favorite album, officers arrived. Then, more. It was a total of 6 police cars before we'd even get to the first interlude (of your favorite album). They found my car rather quickly and surrounded it like they were doing some sort of blueline ritual. I was so busy enjoying the show that I didn't even think that maybe I should go out there. You know, since I called. My phone startled the hell out of me.

"-Yes, Mr. Arrington, the police are outside." she replied.

"I see them. Thank you."

She tried, "ok, don-"

I hung up and walked outside.

"WHOA! WHOA!" they drew their weapons at me. I threw my hands to the sky like the lady in church who tries too hard. Actually, quicker than that.

"STOP!"

Joke was on them because I stopped already, *"I'm the guy who called."*

They yelled, "ARRINGTON!"

"Yes!"

Thankfully they put their weapons down and I felt good about my chances of being able to meet my kids. A few officers returned to their vehicles and one drove off. The others met me at my (beautiful, but scarred) car and its polka-dotted passenger window. They asked me a few questions and 2 police cars drove off. They asked me some more and another car drove off. Then, they asked me another and one more car drove up. Unmarked. It had a killer light system. Cigarette butts flew out of the windows and the questioning officer lost her train of thought. The doors opened and out steps Lattisaw and MeDerra. Same oversized trench coat and MeDerra had that same dumb look while climbing out of the driver's seat.

"Whoa, man," Lattisaw said walking up to the scene. "What the hell is going on in Lafayette?" He extended his hand. "I'm Detective Lattisaw and that's Detective MeDerra."

The questioning officer closed her notepad and gave the two detectives the floor. She looked stargazed, honestly. Like she was standing in front of Prince or Steven Tyler.

"Is this a…joke? What's going on?"

Lattisaw responded, "what do you mean? I mean," he looked at the window and started walking around. "Thank God you weren't in this because it looks pretty serious to me. I don't think this is a joke or… joking matter at all. What do you say?" he asked the questioning officer.

She nodded east to west under his spell.

"MeDerra, get over here and get some pictures," he yelled. "It's our job to keep this neighborhood safe and that's what we're gonna do," he affirmed into my eyes.

He didn't even give me a chance to say anything. Actually, I might have been able to but my tongue and my mind were both tangled in this mystery. It kind of felt like a dream and I just didn't know how to respond to it. When I found the words, he was back in their passenger seat, staring at me. The devilish grin of a sinister child. MeDerra was snapping pictures and humming in the background.

"Hey, officer… Can I uh, have a word with you over here?"

She walked over, "sure thing. What's up?"

"Have you seen these guys before? I think I met them and I'm just-"

She interrupted, "the detectives? I've seen "Meddy" before and I think that one was a transfer. Why? Everything ok?"

"Yeah, I just - think I've seen them before, you know?"

"Understood," she affirmed. "Well, yeah… We've got you covered and they're taking pictures. I'm gonna go grab a few words with security. Kind of… surprised… Like, security didn't come out at all?...Uh, Mr. Arrington?"

I was lost in "Meddy's" goofy eyes. He had finished snapping pictures and was walking backwards to his car with a smirk.

"No. Security didn't come out. No one did."

***

Thing 1 and Thing 2 drove off. Me and the other officer walked into the building and she stopped at the security desk. What a waste of money, that guy. How do you have gunshots on your property and when the responding officers walk up, you're on the phone? Just pitiful. I was thinking about that while I was walking back up to the apartment and it was at that moment that I knew I was going to move us out of Echodale. What a Monday morning, you know? I blame it on the coffee-pizza.

18 LOVE'S ABOUT HONESTY

She said she didn't know what hurt her more, the lies on my tongue or my tongue, telling the lies. Deja had cut me with words before. Never a machete like that. I'm still bleeding from it today. Just blood everywhere. 'Bloody Tuesday' ended up being the name of a drink at StarStrike.

"Gunshots, Austin? Really? Gunshots," she stood at attention with melancholy jazz playing in her pupils. "No. I don't want to hear any-"

She flung a shoe at me and I ducked behind the counter. It was tough because I knew she wasn't herself. You know it, too. I don't even remember what kind of shoe it was, I just remember it hitting the pot on the stove.

"Deja! Calm down!"

Her voice choked me, "don't do that. Na uh! Don't you try to calm…me… DOWN."

Another shoe came flying over the counter top. It yelled up at me, *save yourself, you imbecile!*

Deja carried on, "stop lying! Tell me what's going on!"

"That was yesterday, goddamn'it! A whole yesterday! Like… Baby!"

It got silent. Experts call it the calm before the storm. I heard the staff members of her mind putting a case together for my murder. They wanted me dead. They all wore black pencil skirts with black stiletto heels and those "sexy librarian" glasses. Evil, just sinister. I would much rather deal with the angels that work in Deja's soul than the demons that feed her the lies. Those demons sure know how to stir the pot.

The red lotus thought Bloody Tuesday was the best comedy picture on the marquee. She sat on the floor next to me falling over from the giggles.

Deja's shadow crept over the counter.

> "Wait a minute," she said (well – not really her but the voices and the pregnancy were speaking for her, don't forget that). "Are you and [redacted]...." she spun her pointer finger around in thousands of circles.

It was her little magic wand. I always thought it was cute. A little scary at that particular moment, but she sure did love to wave that finger.

> "Uh-hmph," she continued, "Austin Arrington!"

Mrs. Dortch banged on the wall when Deja hollered my name. If she saw the eyes that I saw, she wouldn't have done such a stupid thing.

> *"What! No!... Baby, seriousl-"*

She interrupted, "I don't know. I know she's not…. That's not her thing, but, shit… What the hell is going on!" Deja began to cry.

I consoled her and the thousands of voices in her head. The whole damn office was crying. My baby was a wreck and I mean, she was right. Wasn't she? We were keeping something from her and that's what happens when you play the game of secrets. People get hurt. To love someone from their hell to their heaven, only to have them leave you in a dark and cold room; that can't feel good. I was protecting her, though. You know that.

***

"So, I told her we might have been mixed up in some shit…"

Apple Pie readjusted herself in one of those god forbidden hospital chairs that are never nice to you. The stiff ones that always have an attitude.

"What? I had to…"

She responded, "I me-, Yeah. I guess…? Or you could have just told her you're helping me with an investigation…Mixed up in some shit? Really?"

She steamed, "Jesus. Scared the shit out of that poor girl," shaking her head, "she's fucking pregnant, man."

The hospital wasn't too far from the airport and my eyes fell in love with a beautiful Airbus. I thought I saw it curl into a heart pattern and sketch me and Deja's initials into the sky. Just like that tree outside of Gape. I got lost in it.

"I'm sorry, I just don't like this. All of this right now is heavy. We're at the hospital," Apple Pie pleaded. "Does she know I'm out here?"

"What? Of course not. She's been back there the whole time… They'ain't even let me back there, yet."

Just as I finished my sentence, doctors came running around the corners. Think Baywatch, but doctors instead of lifeguards. They ran into Deja's room. Me and Apple Pie jumped up as if our other conversation was just an appetizer; the free ones that you can do without.

"What! What's going on?" I pushed into the room.

Deja was hollering from the deepest part of her diaphragm. She tossed and turned in that gurney. Sweat slid down her forehead like rain water and filled the room with tears from the floor to the ceiling. I swam in it with the utmost gratitude for being blessed with a woman like Deja. That glow she was carrying (along with the twins) illuminated the room. I was reminded that God was "in his bag" the day he created the woman.

The circle of life is a merry-go-round that will forever have me in awe. Doctors swooped in to uncover her swollen feet, comforting her every need. She screamed her guts out. I wanted to speak but it wasn't my place.

"What's happening? Eh? Wha- what's going on?" I begged the doctors around me.

One doctor with pale skin and blue marbles for eyes calmed me. Her hand landed on my shoulder like a warm feather. It said, *worry not. Your 'loved' is protected.*

She said, "your wife is going to be fine. Trust me, just wait outside while we try and calm her down. Ok?"

"I mean, what's happening? That's my wife in there."

She responded with a golfer's tongue, "I know, sweetheart. I know. And you've done great being by her side, we know. Right now, the best you can do is wait out here for a few so we can get everything together in there, ok?"

"Hm? Hon?" she continued.

I shook my head but didn't respond. My eyes were so hurt. Deep and hurt.

"The babies are fine and she's fine, ok? We're just having a little moment but everything is fine. Ok? Hm?" Dr. Marble-eyes continued.

I didn't know her but she comforted me. I shook my head. My bottom lip bid her farewell. She rushed back into the room, which had gotten much quieter. I stood in the hallway wearing a cape of unexplained guilt and a crown of concern.

***

The night matured like a 17 year old boy. The waiting room was quiet. I fell asleep watching sports highlights on my phone. I was an emotional wreck. Doctors spent hours ignoring me, telling me that everything was going to be 'ok'. It didn't make it any better that the few times that I stepped into the room myself, Deja was so drugged up, she thought I was everyone but me. She would smile with glossy pupils and frozen corners of her mouth. I could only smile back.

> "Eh, hm, uh… Mr. Arrington," a polite voice woke me out of my sleep. I jumped up. "Mr. Arrington? Hi," she continued. "I'm Dr. Kornian, part of Deja's labor team."

> *"Oh…Yes. Yes- Uh, she's ok, right?"* I paused the highlights.

> She continued, "yes. She's fine. She's been out for oh, maybe two and a half hours now…"

> *"That means I must've been out too."*

> She replied, "Oh yes, definitely. We were thinking we'd have to induce labor earlier and that's probably why you saw all that commotion."

> *"-well, yeah. I kept asking what was going on and everyone was acting-"*

She interrupted, "- I know. I know. It's tough to explain but our first priority is to keep our focus on her in times like this. We were just doing what's best for your wife and your kids, I hope you understand."

I did. You can't really contend with the shitload of plaques on the wall that greet you as you walk into Galloway General, especially the maternity ward. These people know what they're doing but I just wished that they had some care for me too, you know? It was terrorizing watching the chaos from the sideline. You know I don't do the sidelines.

"No. I get it- I… I do. But I just wish, well… I'm just glad everything is ok."

She continued with a silver smile, "yes. Us too. We want to keep her for a few days…Well, until delivery. Her blood pressure climbed and it's really bearing down on the twins and we just want to monitor everything as best we can. She's 'gonna sound a little out of it but it's because she's on some meds. So, no reason to be alarmed."

"- We've just got to keep her pressure down," I looked into my reflection plastered on the stars in the window.

The doctor smiled, "precisely. If you need anything, I'll be at the nurse's station all night. I'll have Debra set you up a cot and uh…Yeah! We're here for you, ok?"

She walked away and my soul felt massaged. I looked at my phone and the muted highlights were rolling. Armonti Perry was down on the hardwood, holding his knee, curled up like a snail in peril.

"Shit, no!"

He had torn his ACL that night. My week from hell had spilled into his. I was starting to wonder if I should just disappear to prevent anyone else from getting struck by lightning. I gathered my things (including my long face) and nestled next to my wife, falling asleep to the 'beeps' and 'beeboops'.

***

Some men wake up to the sounds of roosters singing the sun high. Others wake up to the sounds of garbage trucks and sirens. That next day, I woke up to the sounds of Deja's peaking decibels for help. Loud enough to scare the shit out of her parents. Her mother called at the wrong time. Keep in mind, this is how I was woken up. My poor mind was all over the place. It's equivalent to - have you ever been woken up by a fire alarm in your skyscraper apartment?

***

I rushed to Deja's bedside with her mother on the line. The poor lady was hearing her daughter scream for help as she waited for her rideshare to pick her up from the airport. I was trying to assure her that everything was fine. I hoped she heard the doctors saying the same thing in the background.

"Well, I believe that, uh, this is it," a Doctor said on the other side of the bed. "These kids are ready to go and this body is ready for them to leave."

You know, there was a grin on his face, too. He really liked his job, I could tell. Other doctors swarmed the room, including marble-eyes.

She smiled at me and said, "you're going to be a father."

Why did she say that to me? I would think she knew that tears had a life of their own. They began skydiving down the side of my face and it was the best show in town.

"-Wh…Why is she screaming like that?"

"It's her uterus. The belly is talking to her and she's in pain. Slight pain in the lower back, as well," marble-eyes affirmed. "We've got to watch her blood pressure and vitals, we're a bit ahead of schedule, you know."

"Yes, but everything will be fine, right?"

She affirmed, "we're giving her our absolute best and no matter how long it takes, we'll be by her side for a safe delivery. We've got more equipment coming in and - we'll need some space," she continued as the machines started attacking me. "You can wait right out there, get your loved ones here as fast as you can. We'll call you when it's show time."

So, I slid out of the room. My phone couldn't keep up with my fingers as I called everyone that I could. I started with everyone local. My brother wouldn't make it because he was across the country but he kept calling. He was just trying to be there, you know? I kept telling him that protecting our nation was a pretty good excuse.

My mother and father were supposed to land that morning and her mother was already en route from the airport (I had hoped...She hung on me while Deja was hollering in the background). Duke, Essence, Derry, Jasmine, and the rest of our local friends piled in within 45 minutes, or so. We were all racing against the clock. Those eggs could have hatched at any moment. One could only hope that the queen would try her best to wait for her family to arrive. If you've never been on "baby watch", the best way I could describe it is like when that door opens on the plane and you've got your chute strapped to your back. You're just watching the clouds pass beneath your feet, waiting for your head-diver to yell, "GO! GO! GO!"

A big hand squeezed my shoulder, "ah-hah! My dog! You excited, brotha?"

"Yessir! You already know where I'm at with it."

Duke replied, "facts. This has been - Like, you've been talking about this since what?"

"Since we first met, probably. Not even sure but yeah..."

He replied, "it's probably been that long, honestly. You always wanted to be a dad and man, I'm just fucking proud of you, bruh."

"Uh, ok…. What y'all over here doing? You crying, Duke?" Essence interrupted. "Boy!"

Duke laughed (thank God they weren't arguing that day), "I mean, yeah, I am. Damn. What? You 'gonna tell everyone?"

They proceeded with their usual charade and I couldn't have been more thankful for it. Their voices faded far into the hallway as I noticed Deja's mother plowing into view. She had the momentum of a steam locomotive churning downhill. Her eyes were as concerned as a puppy waiting in the cold, barking at the door and hoping their owner would come rescue them.

"Mom."

She replied, "Oh, Austin!" Those arms comforted me like apple pie fresh out the oven. "Where is she? Where's my girl?"

"Her room's right there. She's probably still 'sleep."

Mom asked, "- What's going on? Sh-she, she's ok, right?"

"Yeah, well. She's good. In some pain. Stomach. Back… W-"

"No, no, I mean. What happened? I'thought they weren't coming for another few weeks," she interrupted.

No matter what, you always yield to a worried mother. Always.

"Her pressure went up at the apartment yesterday and she just looked really... I'don't know. Like, flushed or worn out, or... So, I just threw her in the car and we came here."

She jumped, "-and now we're on baby-watch."

"Babies."

Mom started, "where's the doctor? They still-"

"Oh, um. Over there. That lady with the head wrap... That's her doctor. Well- one of them."

"Ok, thank you, honey. I'll be right back," she started towards the nurses station. "Oh! Those are your friends! Hi, everyone."

Momma Barlow is so sweet. She's always been a joy in my life. The day we buried her was one of the saddest moments in our family. Her legacy lives on. I know it sounds corny but it's true. I wouldn't be sitting here with you as the man I am today without her.

***

So, Duke stole my attention with a purpose. A mission.

He swarmed in as Momma Barlow left me, "whoa, whoa, bro."

"Wassup, man?"

"-Aye man. That Jasmine girl. Who is that?" he asked.

I couldn't help it, *"her name is Jasmine, bro."*

Duke smiled but he didn't laugh. He was serious.

"Nah, it's actually a crazy story. She was our host in Paradise."

Duke replied, "Damn! And she's all the way over here, now?"

"Right. We all became friends. Really good friends. She came over for the baby. Well, babies. Her and Derry are like father and daughter."

"Uh-huh, what y'all over her giggling about?" Essence questioned herself into the conversation. "Especially this one. Don't let him get you in trouble."

"Ain't nobody gettin' nobody in trouble," Duke replied. "That's 'yo problem. Why you always in something you'not supposed to be in?"

She rolled her eyes (I think they're still stuck), "whatever, boy. Austin, you want something from downstairs?"

"No, but thank you though. I do need to eat something. I'm'a go in a few. Thanks though."

She walked off with a bold attitude.

Her hips rocked the waiting room, "oh, you're welcome. Text me if you change your mind."

"Wait! Essy, wait!" Momma Barlow yelled. "Hold on for a second." She was walking over with the doctor and the glow of the early-morning sun. "This is Doctor Braxton-Pa-"

"- Pawton, yes," the Doctor affirmed." (The crowd in my mind began to shout *mar-ble-eyes! mar-ble-eyes!*)

Mom picked up, "Braxton-Pawton, yes. She's on Deja's delivery team and wanted to come over and say hi."

***

They were talking but I wasn't really listening. I knew I should have. I kept staring at Deja's door and the red lotus who was leaning up against it, smacking her gum. This time she had on an all-red set of scrubs and her dreadlocks were blonde with red tips. Her expression was as vanilla as the alphabet and her eyes were as relaxed as Jamaica. I looked at her and she looked at me. She went back into Deja's room with focus.

My phone had been ringing all morning (as you can expect) and I had gotten used to it. So, I stopped looking down at it. But after the red lotus left me, I pulled it out. The same unidentified number had been calling me. The same one from a few days before. You remember that? It just kept saying *Echodale, NY.* There were 28 missed calls, if you can believe that. I remember that number because my mom was born on February 28th. I just tied the two together. What? I'm a momma's boy.

Then, it stopped. No more calls. There were no texts or voicemails. Never anything else. It wasn't Apple Pie because we had been texting all night slash morning. In fact, she was on her way over at the time. Those 28 calls were the last time I would ever be called from that mysterious number and it all made sense by lunchtime.

19 LIGHT OF THE BLUE PEARL

The morning sped by and my little crew never lost steam. Our family laughed and cried through every single second of that glorious morning. Deja was in and out of sleep. Momma Barlow had been spending some time with her and it felt really good to have everyone together, you know? My parents were the last of the bunch but they had landed at E.I. and were headed our way, too.

"Bro," Duke pointed at the TV. "Good fucking riddance."

I looked up and my eyes, man, they were scrolling at that anxiety-inducing cable news ticker. It was Kevlon News and they were reporting that Dale Mangold had officially been executed by the state of New York.

"Fuck that guy, man," Duke said into my confused eyes.

I could see Jasmine, Derry, and Essence talking under their breath in the seats across from me.

The news, "Mangold was tied to a number of heinous crimes including the murder of famed pro basketball prospect, Gerard Penny. He maintained that the draft night murder was - a mistake -"

Everything else just echoed into eternity and had been forgotten as quickly as it had been heard. The weird thing about the death penalty (and, I don't want to get political here - not this interview) is that it doesn't bring back your loved one. It doesn't even really make things seem fair. That's the beauty of life; it cannot be replaced. It can't be exchanged at the counter like soggy french fries or a steak sub with a hair in it. It can't be traded like those little monster cards that all the kids had back in the day. It can only be given or taken away. That's why it should always be appreciated.

> Derry walked over, "you know, lefthand, maybe you should go get yourself a nappy. Er, uh... Go spend some time with your wife in there."

> "Yeah," Duke interjected with the sun on his tongue. "Go ahead and get some sleep, bro. We can keep everybody cool out'here."

I nodded my head and my bottom lip bowed to the gentlemen. I figured an hour, or so wouldn't hurt. It's probably exactly what I needed. I was so exhausted that I couldn't even really digest that headline about Mangold. It should've had a heavier effect on me but I was just tired, man. Surely you would be too after all that I've told you. I looked over at my bride's door and it was glowing gold like the jackpot on a video game. The red lotus had opened the door and poked her head outside. I chased her brown skin like any sensible man would.

I walked into all the 'beeps' and 'beeboops'. It sounded like the International Space Station (the new one they just sent up is magnificent). One of the beautiful things about love is seeing your loved one for the first time in a long time. It had only been a few hours but that feels like eternity in love's arena. It's just like it was in Paradise, watching her walk out of the bathroom with that dress on. Every day with her is special and this was at the top of the list. But I was immediately concerned though.

***

The red lotus was at her bedside, caressing her head so gently; so lovingly. She looked at me as I walked in and looked back into where Deja's eyes would be. Instead, it was her dry eyelids, shielding her from the bright lights of the room. She was sleeping as peacefully as before but there was a tube coming from her mouth. It looked like it traveled forever. It hung out of those juicy lips that I've kissed a million times, and over that shoulder that's been warm rain in the winter, and snow in the summer. The tube disappeared into the salmon-colored wall behind the bed. You could never count how many chords there are in a hospital but I was certain that she had more than before.

A nurse walked in (I called the nurse's station before I even realized I did – I love my wife), "- Mr. Arrington, is everything ok?"

"Uh, well. It just seems like there's more going on here than a few hours ago…"

She replied, "yes, yes. We gave Deja some more meds to help with labor. Her body's trying to decide what to do and it could be a little painful for her. She's fine, though. She's actually doing really well, hon."

"Ok. I just saw the tubes and the-"

She interjected, "- yeah, sure, sure. No. Yeah, the tube just keeps giving her the best oxygen…" she walked over to my sleeping beauty, "…this one here just keeps her hydrated. That's all."

Momma Barlow cracked the door and peeked her head in, "is everything ok?"

The nurse responded while heading for the door, herself, "oh yes, ma'am. Austin just had some questions about what we talked about earlier. I told him Deja's doing well."

She continued, "it's tough to say, right now. But tonight could be the special night. The delivery team is coming back in an hour, or so."

"Oh, wow. Thank you, thank you. Before you go, really quickly. Is there - anything we should… worry about? With the early delivery?"

She responded, "um, I don't believe so. It's nothing that they left me with and… If they were worried, I don't think Dr. Braxton would have left. It's early but we'll be fine."

It was her eyes. They were trying so hard to be confident that I just couldn't trust her. It wasn't anything personal, it's just that my main goal (really, for the rest of my life) is to protect my wife. I was a concerned husband, to say the least. I tried to trust her judgment but couldn't help but hear her struggling to understand it all herself. I believe she could tell that I needed some more information to rest on.

She affirmed on her way out, "once one of them get back, I'll send them right in and they can explain everything for'ya. I'm sure they can give you more than I can. But, if you need anything else, just holler."

The door closed, whispering a light breeze. Red lotus was still bedside caressing Deja's face. I closed the blinds just enough to tell the sun that it was time for this *daddy-to-be* to get a nap. My hands were jittery twisting that tilt wand. The red lotus hissed at me like a lover in a library. I looked over and she extended her arm towards my cot and before you know it, I was resting, dreaming of life without stress.

***

I saw Deja laying on the beach in Paradise. I couldn't see her face, but I know that ass from anywhere and any distance. I would say I was maybe half a mile away, running up the shore to my bride. Life (well, dream-life) was moving slow but the waves were crashing at natural speed. It was as sunny as I could remember. There she was and so were her golden cheeks, bathing in the sun and all of its energy.

"Dej!"

No response. She was asleep.

"Hon?'

She rolled over with a smile and some shades to cover her intoxicated eyes.

She shaded, "baby? Is that you?"

"It's me, boo. I'm here. I saw you over here and I just, ah-Deja."

She smiled, "you make me feel like a little girl. A princess. 'Better stop spoiling me, you know."

"Ah, Deja. You'll always be a girl- "

I never got to finish my statement, man. Her face twisted up and the waves stopped behind me. A chilling stillness covered the beach. Everyone around us had run away. Well, they were running in slow motion. Like, I don't know, imagine if they were running through quicksand with Timberland boots and bulky shoulder pads.

"Ba-bee?"

Deja sat up as fast as a slingshot. Her breasts swelled and convulsed at a remarkable tempo.

"Baby! What's wrong?"

My eyes swam down the shoreline and found the only figure headed in this direction. It was the red lotus. She had on a red, oversized shaw that swayed in a wind, of some sort. The wind was calm where we were sitting. The red lotus's friendship was the least of my worries. I was panicking, man. I needed to know what the hell was going on with my wife. She wasn't saying anything.

Even if she was, I don't think I would have heard it. Everything began to sound like I was listening to it through a toilet paper roll. Or, through those makeshift phones we used to make as kids, the ones with two cans and a string. Even my voice had this hallowed reverb on it. Sounded as if it was getting vacuumed by the atmosphere. The only sound I heard was the one I couldn't stand to hear. This was a dream, sure, but it's a sound that still haunts me. I hated it but couldn't wake from it. It was the sound of my wife forgetting how to breathe. Her faint breath-struggles (add that to the dictionary) flooded my ears like urine down the drain or water in a powerful shower. It hurt - it stank - it stung.

"Deja! Dammit!"

I reached out for her and she didn't reach out for me. Her eyes were facing forward with a focus on the still waters. The red lotus had stopped up shore and that big shaw had gotten bigger, flowing in whatever wind was around her. The ground tickled my feet. It was the sand. I hate sand, man. But it sure was acting as if it loved me that day.

It loved me so much that it started to hug me. The hole in its heart opened towards me like a decrepit witch's mouth at the dentist. It got wider and wider until it reached shoulder-width and then it started to pulsate. I've never been strangled by a boa constrictor (thank God- and, knock on wood), but I imagine this was what my teachers described the feeling to be. Not that they experienced it either, or anything. The pulses were constant and reliable, much like the day at

Le' Gist. That beat. That rhythm. But instead of feeling peace, I only felt pain. There was nowhere to go.

The sand (ew) began swallowing me like the constrictor after strangling its prey - only this time, the prey was still awake.

"Deja!"

I looked upshore and saw how big the red lotus's shaw had gotten. I hoped it would sway towards me; maybe I could grab onto it, you know? Maybe that could help me escape from this crazed lover made of annoying little rocks and minerals. It was sunny where I was drowning (in love) but thunder rumbled above. The red lotus didn't move. Neither did Deja. They were each in their own worlds. Deja was staring straight out over the water and the red lotus was staring straight at me.

"Deja! Please, baby!"

The sand had swallowed just about all of me. My shoulders were bound by the pressure and I tilted my head for the last bit of fresh air. That's when I heard it. Deja's reverberated breathing turned into the loudest, most terrifying scream I've ever heard from my wife. From any human, for that matter. She never turned her head; those eyes didn't even blink. Her jaw looked broken as it hung into the sand, hollering like the 'showoff' soprano in the church choir.

"De-"

As I was reaching out to her, the sand dragged me into its hole. I was covered in darkness from head to toe. Her screams lost their treble and mid-sections. I spent a few seconds in the muffled space before her voice became clear again.

"Austin,' a voice pleaded, "Austin!"

I woke up in the hospital room and Deja's bed was surrounded. She was sitting up holding the doctor's hands, sweating like an influencer who missed their flight to Cabo. I looked at the voice and it was Dr. Kornian.

> "Mr. Arrington, it's time," she said calmly. I'm not sure if it was her voice or her eyes that did it, but I was at peace.

"I'm coming, baby!"

***

Kornian handed me a set of baby-blue scrubs and this medical-hat thing (I guess they didn't want me to infect the baby, I mean kids, with my balding hair follicles - listen, I don't blame them). All of that is still in my office closet today. You never lose those things but I disagree with the parents who say the first is always special. I think they all are.

I reached to the tray next to the bed and gloved myself with the blue latex. Deja looked over at me like she was coming back to her corner after fighting 6 rounds with Laila Ali. The heavy breathing, the sweat, the battle-face; it was all there.

You know what else was there? Me. I was fully present and my bride knew that. That's why she smiled at me like she did. I extended both hands to her and she let go of the doctor's. She grabbed (the hell out of) mine and got back into that game-face; the grit of motherhood and childbirth. Man, what a woman. We pushed and pulled until we heard a crying infant come out of her vagina. Then, we pushed and pulled some more until we heard a second. I guess it really was there.

Then it was us, all of us, who were crying. It was the most beautiful day of my life.

20 Everyone's a Liar

"James and… James and Germany," Deja told the doctor.

I laughed a little bit because I didn't know why she hesitated. We only had the *what're we naming these things* conversation a million and two times.

"J.J and G.G."

She rolled her eyes at me as if it were the worst nicknames she'd ever heard. My dad jokes were ahead of schedule and I was a happy camper.

"Look at those eyes, so-bwight… Yes they are," Momma Barlow leaned into the twins.

Dr. Korninan smiled, "yes, they sure are. You guys did good."

"-Ah! Yes you did!" charmed a deep voice into the room. One of those voices that swallow the air around it. Like a grenade going off right by your ear. "I heard the news and I just had to stop by."

It was the creepy, big doctor (-esque) guy from before. He was wearing the same lab coat and his skin still looked desert-parched.

He continued, "Austin and Deja! The Arringtons! Aw, let me see! Let me see!"

"Dr. Calloway! Hi, sir!" Deja hollered out.

I looked at her with the most puzzled gaze. I had realized that he was part of her birthing team. Took me a second to process. I found it weird that he wasn't around too much after that. What about you? Don't you find that weird? I sure as hell did. And, I sure as hell didn't want him touching my kids.

"Whoa, wait."

Deja was confused, "Austin… What's wrong?" Her eyes were saying *uh, what?*

Scary Calloway chimed in, "yes, Mr. Arrington. What's wrong?"

It wasn't just him, though. It was the whole room. Everyone was staring at me as if I had unplugged the turntables at brunch.

"Babe?" Deja questioned.

I sank a corner of my mouth. The red lotus stood up from her chair. Her face was much more gritty than mine. She extended her hand as if she was hailing a cab in Utah; calm and unashamed. There was no pressure to risk her life for attention. But, her eyes, man. Her eyes were falling as cloudy as a Wednesday in Seattle (without that delicious coffee, of course). She couldn't bear to look at me any longer and turned her head but kept her arm extended.

> "Son? You ok?" my mother said to me with her hand on my shoulder.

My dad (a veteran like my brother and everyone else except for me) stood at attention. I looked back at Scary Calloway who had his hands out for my kids.

> *"Yeah, I'm fine. I'm fine. Just had- I don't know. Sorry about that, doc."*

That's what my mouth said but my eyes said something different. I can't even really get into that conversation because I don't think you would understand. It's nothing personal, please don't take it as such. But Scary Calloway understood and he understood it well. That was the moment I think we had a mutual understanding that something fishy was going on and I wasn't an inattentive seaman.

> He smirked back, "aw, yes! Welcome to fatherhood, Austin. Always on guard."

The babies started to cry.

> "Now, now," Scary Calloway said as he began to embrace them, "sh! Sh! Uncle M has you."

Ah, that shit grinds my gears even thinking about it today. Apple Pie knew that something was going on, too. She stood in the corner, near the red lotus, hanging by the window like a R&B video. Apple Pie cut those sweet eyes at me across the room; cinnamon sugar and all. We stared at each other as if we were the tightrope act in the circus; focus is lifesaving, don't forget that. I looked at Derry and he was on our wavelength as well. His eyes were trying to join the conversation. When you're loved, you're loved. What can I say? I never felt alone after Paradise. My circle has always been there and they certainly were there that day.

My father, what a guy. One of the toughest nails to hammer into the foundation. He's been like that my whole life. He had a sweet spot for Deja, but I think she just knows how to bring that out of everyone. She's a sweet girl. But my dad, though, his eyes were trying to butt in on that conversation too. I let him in but Apple Pie and Derry didn't. I didn't expect them to. He's my dad and he was with me. I think he knew that look of a worried father all too well, especially after trying to keep up with my wild childhood. Me and Devin were, just... That's another story for another day.

"Hey, uh... Austin?" Scary Calloway spoke. "I've got something for you. I'always got something for my new fathers. From our team, here."

My eyes circled the room at the doctors and their scrubs. I saw it as camouflage for whatever reason. One of those *no one can be trusted* moments.

He waved, "say we take a walk?"

He was already making his way to the door and didn't leave me much room to decide if it was a good idea.

My circle had their reservations, too. I put those concerns to rest and made a quick decision that I was going to follow Calloway. Scary, or not, it was me and him.

***

Our footsteps swallowed the busy halls of the maternity ward. A lot sex was being had in Echodale, let's just say that. Or, a lot of love was being made. I like that better. Me and the big guy didn't say two words to each other the whole way. We both were walking with a purpose, like two lovers just trying to make it to privacy for some adult behavior. Even in the elevator, we just stood there watching the floors pass by. He did speak to other doctors at the stations as we passed them; a doctor, a Mayor, and a fucking creep.

> "Mis-ter-Arr-ing-ton," he said as he nestled behind his desk. "I don't think I ever told you how much of a fan I was watching you'guys at State."

I stood in silence and left the door open. Sounds of the busy corridor kept me company.

> He pointed to the empty chair across from him, "please."

The open door didn't bother him so I didn't let the moment bother me.

> He jabbered, "ah! You're going to be a dad! How fun?"

He was as excited as a pyro at the harbor on independence day. His shoulders scrunched up and he was sitting on his hands, like a wife who just found out that she was going on an all-expense paid shopping spree, courtesy of hubby. Actually, it didn't matter who paid for it. Never does.

"Please, tell me. Are you excited?" Scary Calloway continued.

"Ahem. -um, well. I just... I think that word might be a bit of an understatement."

He replied, "ah. I see. Well, I've got two of them. A brute and a bitch. Enjoy these early moments because, kid, when they become adults..." His eyes finished the sentence and his floating hand joined in to help. "You know."

"Hmph. Still a blessing, I think. Right?"

He replied, "oh yes. Hell yes! The memories always make everything worth it, you know? Bad day? I think about them. Good day? I think about them. It's just when they get older it seems like that whole rule about the stove and putting your hand up there, you know? It just goes out the window. Then - Then- watch this, then you become more of a firefighter or something. Or... or, a doctor? How about that?"

"Well, yeah. That's what I think makes parenting, you know, parents... That's what makes them, us, heroes."

He fell back into his chair with the veins screaming for help through his lifeless skin, "well, by goodness. I'll be damned. Now, that's a thought, kid."

We paused. Our eyes were locked in a draw straight out of a western movie, one of those Chip Dalen films with the corny music and tumbleweeds. It was just air floating around us trying to decide how to address the tension in the room. There were so many factors at play: he's creepy, the door's open, we're joking about parenthood (although I didn't much like the "Brute and the Bitch" statement), he's connected to Jane Doe and that weird ass morgue somehow. I didn't know how but I knew something was up with him.

"Oh," he interjected, "and this," he reached down into his drawer, "this- is for you, my friend."

It was a dozen cigars. Half wrapped in pink ribbon and the other half wrapped in blue.

"Full disclosure, they were all blue until last week," he laughed to himself.

I didn't know what to say so my mother and her manners spoke for me.

"Thank you, man. Wow."

He leaned back again, "hey. Don't mention it, kid."

The air in the room was interviewing us both. It has to take note of the tension! That's what air does. It was working in overdrive and sweating, like a transcriber during the Insurrection hearing. Every word and emotion had to be right, or else. Scary Calloway hopped up, breaking the silence once again. I got up, too.

"No, no," he pleaded as he walked to the door. "You just sit right there and relax for a second. We'll go back up in a minute."

He closed the door as politely as a principal getting ready to tell a parent that her son will be suspended.

"Oh, ok..."

He continued, "there's something I need from you, son."

"How...can I help you, Dr. Calloway?"

He took a deep breath and began scrolling through his phone.

"Stop this shit," he slammed it on the desk in front of me and flipped it so I could see.

It was the surveillance footage of me and Apple Pie pulling the sheets back from over the stiffs. It had audio and everything. I swear I heard the smiling asian laughing. I'm not much of a passive aggressive person so I faced it head-on; with silence, a guilty silence.

"You and your little friend, Miss [redacted], need to stay away," he sat on the corner of his desk. "The goal is not just to bring the little ones into the world but… to be around to watch them grow into the little parasites they become."

Ah, that evil grin still haunts the hell out of me. Pardon me.

"Um. Is that a threat?"

He affirmed into my eyes, "yes. Yes, it is."

"You were mixed up in something you shouldn't have been," he continued, parading around the room. "And now, you're going to mix yourself right out of it. It's a threat… A warning," he turned to me slowly, "a promise."

His smile was ice cold but his temple was steaming. My heart was dancing at a deadly disco.

Dr. Calloway to ER1, Dr. Calloway to ER1, 2-7-0.

"And that's my ride," his pointer finger reached for the ceiling. "Go on! Go enjoy your kids, man. This day is special! Remember, it's important to be there for them every step of the way."

***

He led me out of his office and I walked through thousands of corridors to get back to my wife and kids. My palms were so damn sweaty, I almost dropped the box of cigars. I had on these brown dress boots with blue khakis, topped with a white tee shirt. It didn't look too bad in my reflection on the elevator's steel doors. But then, 3 bullet holes appeared on the shirt and blood started drowning the cotton. It was freaking me the hell out! I started panicking (and doing a mild man-scream, sounds more like a half-hearted grunt), wiping my chest as quick as windshield wipers in a hurricane. The doors opened and fell against the wall. I touched all over my chest to make sure I was dreaming. My respiratory system needed some more time to bounce back.

"Austin! You... You good, boo?" questioned Essence.

She had trays of food in her hands and a piece of celery hanging from her lips.

"Yeah, I'm fine. I'm fine. What you got there?"

Essence smiled, "it's just some wings. You sure you good...Right? You look kinda, you know..."

The red lotus appeared in the back of the elevator and her hand crawled onto mine.

"Essy... Ye-"

The damn doors started closing. I was glad they did though. I jumped up to push the button again so I wouldn't end up on another floor, or something. It forced me to get off the wall and back into gear.

***

THE OTHER BLUE

I walked back into the room and everything was golden. Fireworks were going off just below the ceiling and time was mudding along. There was upbeat classical music blaring overhead, at least that's what I heard. Jubilee. Joy. You wouldn't survive the emotion of it all, it was just beautiful. But, I won't bore you with it. I know what this is about. We'll save that for later.

***

I nudged Apple Pie (who was that one person not dancing at the party, you know the one). We hurried down to the parking garage and I remember Deja cutting her eyes at us as we walked out.

"Did you get it?"

Apple Pie closed her door, "get what?"

"The voice note... I just sent it. Well, maybe like - 30 minutes ago, or something."

She pleaded, "What? Er... No, I..."

"Ugh. Don't worry about it, just chill. Just chill...- Listen," I spun the phone between us.

We leaned into the center of the car, just above the middle console. Honestly, that was completely unnecessary. I feel like we only did it because we were really invested. I could tell that I had dragged Apple Pie into a great mystery and that's the kind of shit that turns her on.

"No fucking way," she looked at me with those big curious eyes. "Did he just threaten you?"

She didn't want a response. I know because she didn't wait around for one. By the time I realized it, she was halfway out of the car and on her way to find Scary Calloway.

"Wait, [redacted]. Stop. Just stop…Come- come back. Sit down."

She leaned down but kept her torso out of the car, "Austin, he threatened you. What the fuck? I'm going back."

I hopped out because she wasn't coming back in.

"[Redacted]! Stop. You know better than me that this'ain't 'gonna solve nothing. Not like this."

My voice echoed a bit and I didn't like it. I just didn't know how far it would carry, you know? I looked for it but found nothing. I was looking for the red lotus as well. She was nowhere to be found.

Apple Pie turned her head, "shh. That was loud."

I put both of my hands up a few inches like a hidden surrender. My eyebrows followed suit. She slid back into the car. We sat there for a few seconds, breathing as heavy as two lovers the morning after the honeymoon.

"Play it again," she broke the silence.

"What a maniac," she continued. "All that smiling and cute shit he does, charming. Then he makes a cold threat against you. Wasn't even hesitant or anything. Like," she turned to me in a feminine tone, "what are we in right now, Austin? The'hell is going on?"

***

All of this is in the book and it's crazy to be talking about it like this today. I had no clue what Project Cold Wednesday was going to become. Sitting in that car with Apple Pie, it wasn't on my mind, either. I was a father for the first time. I felt like my life wasn't my own, in so many ways. Pity is a horse that I ride with my hands tied behind my back. One can only hope that it has your best interest at heart.

21 Business is About the Village

Deja slept in my arms. We squeezed into that hospital bed and fell asleep watching the twins on the monitor. I got up a couple times throughout the night to go see them myself. The red lotus came with me and I was happy to have her. I thought she had left me in that parking garage.

My forehead kissed the cold glass of the nursery and she leaned on my shoulder. She grabbed my hand and placed it on her belly, I rubbed it and whatever jewel was inside. She smiled at me and I smiled at the twins.

"No," I smiled at the red lotus.

"I'm sorry?" a nurse passed by.

"Oh, nothing. Nothing. Sorry about that. Thinking out loud."

She smiled, "no worries. Hey, I know you."

"Hi, I'm Austin."

She replied, "Austin! Yes. Nice to meet you, I'm Kerry." "Which one is yours?"

"Well, I'm lucky enough to have two. There they are, hi guys."

"Ah, twins! You are lucky! Aw… That one's got those eyes on you," she said in this baby-jabber talk.

You know that damned language that nobody speaks until you have a kid. It makes everyone talk like an alien trying to learn the English language with extra-nutty peanut butter in their mouth. It's cute though. Well, until it's not.

***

Those 'eyes' that she spoke of were James's and he wasn't looking at me, he was looking at the red lotus. I could hear her swooning the kid behind me while I was making small talk with that nurse. Within a few moments, I was down the hall and back in the hospital bed with my wife in my arms.

You may remember the story but Deja was kept in the hospital for quite some time after the twins were born. Her vitals were usually well, but with the newfound diabetes and the increase of stress (which we never identified the source of), doctors were worried about her. I wasn't though. She told me she was good and I believed her. I always do. She started blogging on the News Station's website about her motherhood experience and the city was falling even deeper in love with my Deja. She also wrote that phenomenal piece about Houston's star Quarterback and his battle with social anxiety, written from that hospital bed. What a girl, I tell you. The twins just seemed to make life better for her.

***

"Your wife is quite the scribe, yes?" Derry said from the corner of my office. "Her stomach's still swollen, she's barely got a voice, and here she is writing - writing wonderfully. Tsk."

His brown-framed (thick) glasses fell to the floor.

> *"Yes sir! That makes one of us. She always said I would work for her one day."*

He reorganized himself, "ah, don't be silly, lefthand. You're quite the sparkle too, eh? Tell me. What came about of that… $20,000 from that Perry fellow?"

> *"Well, he wanted to hold on the project but he wouldn't take the money back. Something's up-"*

"Ah, yes," he said, fiddling around the room.

> *"Actually, I need to text him. You know he got hurt again the other night?"*

Derry hesitated. His mind was in the cosmos somewhere, ice skating with his far thoughts.

He continued, "I'm sorry, again?"

> *"Armonti. He tore his knee up the other night."*

"A pity. Just a shame," he uttered, "you know? That $20,000. I think I want to triple that."

I was shuffling papers around my (unbelievably junky) table when he said it. Imagine getting to the end of your favorite box of cookies, reaching in that desolate plastic and mysteriously, there's more. We know Derry to be a man of great wealth, that's no secret. I had also come to know him as very generous by then. But, I didn't know how to describe this particular gesture.

"In fact," he continued before arriving at the table, "I want to triple that every quarter. And - lefthand, I want to stay by your'side. Right there, yeah? I would like to serve-"

"Derry… Derry. Let's, just… Let's. Wait a minute. What're you-"

He affirmed, "-I'm saying I want to help your dreams come true, lefthand. The new ones. Please, take the money. Take my hand. Yeah?"

He sat there across from me, watching my eyes try their hardest to keep the clouds tight. The rain was dying to fall. I just couldn't hold it in anymore. No one knows about those tears, except for him.

"Ah, my boy. Yes, yes, to'be emotional is to be free, my boy," he consoled me. "You're a light who deserves to be believed in.

"But.." I pushed myself away, *"I don't get it. What-exactly is it that you believe in?"*

His eyebrows left the room. His mouth turned its corners.

"Well, truthfully," he said, making his way around the room again. "Truthfully, I don't quite know."

It got quiet.

"It's not so much a matter of 'what'. I think this one is more about the who," he affirmed over his shoulder.

We made eye contact in an exchange of brotherly love.

"Thank you."

"Yes, thank you. I want to serve and build things. You're allowing me to do that," his hand rested on my shoulder. "But, we must first speak of some things."

"Yeah, sure."

Derry led, "I know we've got that documentary picture but there's something else you're cooking. You and that polizia."

Another tricky thing about Derry is his magnetism with people and information. Things just seem to flow to him and he sees the world through the lens of the Matrix-esque code that it's built from. He can read between lines, seeing the hidden as clear as a new wine glass. Hearing the unspoken as clear as rolling thunder in an open field. I leaned back in that cheap chair and squinted my eyes at him. They squinted right back at me.

"Tell you what, would you like some coffee?"

THE OTHER BLUE

Of course he did. Who doesn't want that shit? We sat there and sipped away. I told him about Project Cold Wednesday and his jaw slid down his torso. It rested on the floor like a dog after a day at the beach.

22 CHECK YOUR MAIL

Was he scared? I don't know, probably. He was doing a good job hiding it though. We were quite the talkative bunch heading back to the hospital. I gave him a synopsis of who (and how badass) Apple Pie was. You know what? Actually, no, he wasn't scared. He seemed kind of thrilled by it all. He stuck by his desire to serve. The entire time, he was just focused on how he could be of assistance. He was very keen on not getting into any mess, though.

***

The plan was to meet Apple Pie at the hospital and go from there. You might be wondering why we would do such a thing considering "Scary Calloway", but family comes first. My wife and kids top of the "non-negotiables" list.

"Ba-by?"

"Yes," I heard her from the corner of the room. "Hi, husband."

She revealed herself from the shadows, planting a kiss on my lips as if I was the prize.

"You're like, up, up?"

She continued, "Yeah, I'm up, up. They're saying I can go home."

Momma Barlow came in, "Deja, honey. Oh! Hi, son!" She planted a kiss on my cheek as if I was a prize. "Look at our girl."

"The most beautiful girl I've ever seen."

Deja got bashful (she always did but she really was a ham, don't believe her), "oh, stop it. They're bringing the twins in here in a minute and then I guess we can go."

"Ok," I nodded, *"but, why didn't you tell me?"*

Deja stared, "well.. Hon… I tried to call, see?"

She wasn't lying. She called me 4 times but it never rang. You know? She thought I was lying about that for quite some time.

"Oh, wow. Sorry about that. I mean, you see I've got nothing on here."

The door slid open, "that's ok. It happens all the time. These new phones."

It was Scary Calloway, holding the twins with a nurse not too far behind him.

He scratched some more, "miscommunication and all of that jazz. These damned things have a mind of their own."

237

He clenched the twins tighter, "Oops! I've got to watch my mouth. We've got younglings around."

Everyone laughed except me. Not only was it not funny but what was he doing with my kids in his hands? I didn't like it. He handed them to the nurse who began prepping them for their first real-world experience.

"Aht! Aht!" he wagged at Deja, "you cannot walk out of here like that, Mrs. Arrington. Please."

Another nurse wheeled in a wheelchair (duh) and pleaded for Deja to hop in. You know Deja so you know that wasn't easy. To her credit, she was looking quite stronger than most of what my imagination had created. I was just sure that the whole childbirth thing was going to cripple her for some time but she was bouncing around the room as if nothing happened.

They'll listen if you beg enough, though. Talking about wives. She sat in the wheelchair with the look of a disappointed kid on Christmas. That is until she had the twins along for the ride.

The car was tight but we were as happy as a divorced woman on vacation in Jamaica, swinging her feet on the beach, smiling at life ahead. Deja rode in the backseat. The red lotus kept me company up front. I kept looking at my family in the mirror, smiling like a coat with a new button.

We got home and Deja went right to sleep. I spent a few hours taking care of the twins. They slept a lot too. I must admit, it is exhausting adjusting to this 'brave new world'. I tried my hardest to let them sleep but I found myself digging in their bassinets like the obese in a cookie jar.

THE OTHER BLUE

***

When I wasn't bothering the twins I was typing away on the phone. Apple Pie had been grinding her gears on the case. We spoke about it at the hospital, briefly, but plans got thrown off when Deja was discharged. It was earlier than expected but we needed it. Deja's the tidy one and the apartment definitely missed her. Our counter had piled up from days of mail (what? We were a little busy, you know). I started sifting through it all while I was waiting for a reply and there it was; tattered and mangled, kind of open too. A letter addressed to me from the New York State Penitentiary. It was from Dale.

"What!"

I stared at that thing with anger in my eyes and sorrow in my heart. His name just brings me back to the only murder I've ever witnessed in my life. The only one, still, to this day. It just so happens that it was my best friend and the hole in my heart still bleeds.

"Shit."

I caved to curiosity and opened the letter. It was coming from the clink so I figured it wasn't a bomb or a chemical substance, or some sort. I know you're probably like *why did he open it? No!* You would have, too.

It was a slow-rip. The envelope let out this putrid scent of Vienna sausages and batteries. Maybe a hint of cigarette smoke, too. His handwriting was some of the most beautiful script I'd ever seen. He drew the letters with precision and grace, a delicate grip of the pen. His first line was chilling: *they probably killed me already.*

It took the breath out of my body. I slid down the wall and sat on the floor to read the rest of it. He found himself on death row (I didn't even know) after a string of murders had been tied to him by his DNA. Like most others, he maintained his plea of innocence and was uncomfortable with his death sentence. He assured me that the only murder he'd actually committed was Gerard's draft night. He apologized for that grim evening. A cold breeze whisked its way through the apartment and the red lotus sat next to me, rubbing my shoulder and the blood boiling in it. The rest of the letter was two pages of his final words but the last paragraph was a needed piece of the puzzle.

***

He asked me for a favor. He assured me that those murders he'd been tied to were all connected. He wanted me to look into it. I was the closest thing to the media that he knew of, someone who knew he existed, if you will. I folded that scented (ew) letter up and stuck it on the counter overhead. It was me and the red lotus on the floor, again. Looking at one another with upside-down universes in our eyes. Deja came and got the kids, I went and got some sleep.

***

The next morning, I woke up to crying twins and my wife pacing the floor. Day 2 of the 'daddy-chronicles'. Wouldn't trade it for the world.

Deja sent me to the market for some items for our kingdom. I walked. I hated driving her car, honestly. Nothing wrong with it. I mean, it's just not mine, you know? I couldn't wait to get that damned window repaired.

"Austin!" Perry said. He had called a few minutes after I walked out of the building.

"AP, wassup man?"

He smiled, "no one's called me that in a long time. I'm cool, bro. Taking care of this leg."

"Yeah, man. Sorry about that. We were in labor when it happened, I meant to-"

"Hell yeah! That's right! Congratulations, brother," he interjected. "Yes sir, yes sir!"

Small talk became big talk.

He continued, "listen, man, the… weirdest shit, bro. You know Sidney'sister you was asking about?"

"Yeah."

He continued, "dude, she's missing. It's crazy because, like, we literally were just talking about her."

I stopped in my tracks and brought the phone closer to my face.

"Bro, what? She's missing?"

"Yeah, dude," he replied, "- Bro, look that shit up. It's trending right now. At least over'here."

"Wow."

He carried on about the case and then started talking about his documentary. That's when we ironed out some of the final details and decided we were going to resume production.

I walked in circles around that damn grocery store. You know how it is trying to shop with the world weighing on your mind. It's tough. You'd have better luck blindfolded in a maze at the pumpkin patch. I scrolled through the trending posts while I was standing in line behind this tiny white woman.

She kept staring with goofy eyes until finally she said something, "new father?"

"Ha, yes."

She smiled back at me, "congratulations! You do anything to protect them. They're your only slice of heaven. Boy or girl?"

"Thank you. Both, actually. Twins."

She replied, "oh, what a blessing. Congratulations."

"Ah, thanks-"

***

My phone rang and it was Apple Pie. I wish you could have heard her voice. She was whispering but very aggressive, you know? Like a really mad investigator descending on a target in the middle of a funeral. The quiet part of the service, too. Like during prayer, or something. I sent her a few threads of the missing 'white woman of the day' and she remembered exactly who that was.

"This is the girl you showed me that night! That Sid-girl's sister. Whoa," she whispered. "That mean's Perry's-"

"He's the one that told me."

Deja was resting with the twins on her breasts. I snuck into the apartment and snuck out, as quick as a thief in a convenient store. Apple Pie picked me up shortly thereafter.

***

"Wait," she said as she was turning out of the crowded lot, "you hear that?"

"Oh. Yes. It's me. Well, my phone…"

She looked over, "oh…ok?"

"It's just Derry," I affirmed, *"he's in."*

You could hear him cackling like a seasoned smoker in the background. He took over and re-introduced himself to Apple Pie. Derry was extremely wealthy but the man loved to serve. It was unbelievable how quickly he got into gear. It took her a while to warm up to having him by my side but she realized our partnership and began to trust him.

She said, "wait here."

"Uh... Where are you going?"

"To go do some damned police work. I'm tired of playing around. Just keep an ear out on the line and if you hear anything wild, well, yeah. Make sure you're recording everything, too," she continued.

Before I could tell her how much of a bad idea I thought it was, she left. It was really dramatic, too, with her black dress pants dawning her heels. Footsteps echoed through the garage until she disappeared into the stairwell.

Derry replied, "and now, we wait, lefthand."

She made her way to Calloway's door. It took her no time. He let her right in. We had our ears in the room, right there with them.

"Dr. Calloway, I'm Detective [redacted]," she said. It was a hollow sound, a little faint, but we heard her. "I wanted to see-"

He interrupted, "I remember you. Never had the pleasure, though. Please, take a seat."

Then we heard the door close right behind his last word. Apple Pie was nestling herself into her chair and we heard the skin trying to get comfortable. Like a butt-dial situation, you ever get one of those calls? It was like that. Just trying to paint the picture, here.

"You're part of the Arrington delivery, that's where I've seen that face," Scary Calloway warmed. "That Austin is one of my favorites."

She replied, "Yeah, he's a good guy. One of mine, too. Speaking of which, he was called down here to ID a woman a few weeks back. This face look familiar?"

"Somehow, I knew you were going to ask me about that, detective," he said as we heard footsteps shuffling.

He must've been wearing some of those hard-soled dress shoes that slide across the room, turning the dusty floors into an instrument.

He continued, "let's have a look, again."

It fell silent on the line.

"Beautiful woman. I won't shit you, none. I know her. She was right downstairs," he responded. I could hear his smile. "She came into my morgue here and we took care of it all."

Apple Pie responded, "Well, are you aware this is a missing persons case?" Paper shuffled in the background. "But, I guess…. I guess this isn't a missing persons case anymore if you're saying you saw this woman in your morgue, right?"

"No. It's a missing person's case, right now," he replied. "And I intend on keeping it that way."

It was silent for a few seconds before the sound of one of them striking the other. A heavy punch. Think comic sound effects from the 70s or the dramatic grunts of a wrestling match. But, it was only one punch. Then nothing.

"Shit."

"[Redacted]! Yo!"

Derry interjected, "I'm pretty sure that's not anything good, lefthand."

"Yeah?"

He replied, "you should get out of there and we'll figure it out...I... maybe just out of that garage."

"I can't leave her. Ok, do me a favor... Save that file and then record again when it's done."

He replied, "already saving, lefthand. It'll be in the cloud thing..."

I tried to get her attention again, *"[Redacted]!"* To no avail. The line was quiet. "Shit, man. [Redacted]!"

The door across the parking garage swung open, loud and painful. His lab coat fluttered from the door's wind and he stood there in a frantic search for company. I presume he was looking for me.

"Shit, shit, shit. Derry, he's right here."

He replied, "oh, dear. You'd do your best to melt into that seat, lefthand."

I slid down in the passenger seat and leaned over the middle compartment. It was silent. Only sound was the busy 195-Freeway climbing over the garage's walls. I leaned up just enough to see if danger was still there. That scary son-of-a-bitch was standing there with his eyes on his phone. Then he looked up in my direction and I knew something was wrong.

"Oh, shit. He's coming."

Derry replied, "ok, now you've got to get out of there."

I climbed into the driver's seat and pushed the start. He appeared in the side mirror, just close enough to be seen but still at a fair distance. He wasn't moving with any speed, really. Very casual in the pursuit. It was so weird. I noticed that his face was painted with a devilish grin the more he came into view.

"I think this man is enjoying this."

Derry replied, "well, we're not, lefthand. Get out of there."

He was as calm as the Santa Monica shore in the morning.

I sped out of the garage and he let me leave. I was thinking there'd be someone chasing me or at least Scary Calloway doing a brisk jog but there was none of that. No fanfare or antics. Apple Pie was in trouble. We kept the line open and Derry recorded it all. I didn't go far and I swore that I wouldn't leave the property without her. Unfortunately, I would have no choice because she never came out and I never went in. I sat across the street just waiting for a word from her. We kept calling out for her and she never responded. Then we heard sounds of violent ruffling before the audio got really clear.

We heard a small chuckle before the line went dead. It beeped as if we had been disconnected.

"I think she's gone," Derry said.

It was Jacob. That's who crossed my mind. Him reaching out for Apple Pie and her not being there.

***

A half-hour later, I hopped out and crossed the street without a bashful streak. The red lotus was with me. We marched to the help desk who led us to Scary Calloway's office. I knocked 7 times before he rushed to the door. You'd think he'd be harder to find after what transpired here earlier. Or, at least a little bit of worry across his face. That's when I saw it. His right eye had a gash as fresh as the first cup of coffee.

"Austin, please come in," said Calloway.

"Where is she?"

"I'm right here," said Apple Pie. "I'm right here."

"[Redacted]! Let's get the hell out of here-"

The door closed behind me.

"Please," Scary Calloway said. "We need to talk about something."

Apple Pie's eyes led me to the chair, "Yeah, you need to hear this. Just- yeah."

"No, we've got to go!"

"She could have left a while ago," Calloway affirmed. "But she chose to stay here with me and- and- hear what I have to share. After she woke up, of course."

That explained the syringe on the floor.

***

We sat at his desk. I was steaming at the see-saw of it all. I just wanted to get back to my family and protect my home, you know?

"-I'll tell you like I told her," Calloway said, "all of this is beyond the three of us. We've gotten mixed up in each other's mess… those damn webs got'tangled. But at the end of the day," he stood up, "not one of us knows what the hell is going on."

I turned to Apple Pie, *"what's going on?"*

"I just told you," Calloway grew frustrated. "It's beyond all of us. We take care of a few things here and there for EPD and that's it-"

"-And I work there and know nothing about it," Apple Pie chimed. I was upset and I jumped out of my chair.

"No. What about that threat to me earlier?"

Scary Calloway replied, "kid, I'm just trying to protect my staff. That's what I was sworn to do. Protect this staff and protect that morgue. I don't want to hurt you."

"But- what about those... detectives? and ... those officers down there?"

Calloway walked over to me, "kid, listen. Those aren't our guys! Hell, she's an officer, I mean that's obvious. I'thought they were all with you. I mean, I just see you all sneaking around the morgue - all the time, I don't know."

"Those guards down there, Austin-," Apple Pie led.

Calloway continued, "-they're a whole different company than Locke. That's who handles security up'here." "All I want is for y'all to stay out of that basement, ok? I don't want any trouble. I can't handle it, frankly. I'm a doctor, ok? Not this," Calloway began waving his hands, "-this."

"I don't think you understand, I was the one called down here to see that lady. I… I can't get it out of my head!"

Calloway replied, "well, I need you to, Ok? I don't know why you were even brought into this, ok? Just leave everything alone and let those detectives handle it, ok?"

"You just don't mess with these people," he continued. "-things I'seen, you just - leave them alone. That morgue operates with a mind of its own and we just have to leave that alone. They'said you just always protect your morgue so that's what I'm doing. I'm begging you, please leave it alone. Let those guys handle it."

He pointed at us, "Jacob, Mrs. Arrington, the twins, and my'gang. Let's just leave this alone."

She looked at me before rising, "yeah, Calloway. We're going to leave this one alone."

I didn't have much room for a response and the little space that I did have was occupied by sheer shock.

"What're we doing? We can't give up on this," I whispered to Apple Pie in the hallway.

She affirmed, "listen, Austin. There are some things that are just beyond us. That's just the way this'thing works now. All these bureaus and divisions, it's a mess. It can be shitty, sometimes. Maybe - maybe in the old days, you know? Maybe back then I would chase after it but we've got a lot to lose. This is just - let's just let them handle it."

"Fine. Fuck."

I was just tired of hearing about it. The merry-go-round made me dizzy. Out of all the people involved, I was the layman in the group. It felt foolish and pointless to keep opposing Apple Pie. My chest felt as soft as fresh pancakes. My will to fight had melted like butter. I dissolved into surrender and had taken my first steps towards forgetting the whole thing.

It's good I didn't actually forget, huh? Beyond the money that Project Cold Wednesday made me, think about the impact it had. You know?

23 THE MONEY MINDSET

"Deja, honey?" I walked into my apartment. *"Yo! Th'fuck? Deja!"*

They were sitting on my couch. Lattisaw and MeDerra.

Lattisaw got up, "Austin, Austin. Shhh! Calm down. Don't want the neighbors to think something's wrong."

I didn't even respond. I started high-stepping through my apartment, looking for my wife and kids.

"The fuck did you do?"

"Austin. They are fine. They weren't here when we got here. Promise," he responded. His coat tail slid back, revealing his revolver. It bowed. "-Call her then."

I did.

"Hey babe…Where'd you go?"

Deja responded (she sounded so happy, too. It brought me peace to hear her voice), "we ran out of tissue and -"

Honestly, I didn't even pay attention to the rest of what she was saying. I was happy to hear her voice and know that she's safe but still… thrown off. Significantly. In fact, my life had become one really-long curveball; with a mind of its own. I didn't want to startle her so I didn't tell her. I called Derry soon after we got off the phone and told him to "bump into her". Just to keep her safe.

"You done?" questioned Lattisaw, "can we just talk now? All of your people are safe."

"No! I don't want to talk," I stormed into my family room. *"I just want all of this shit to be over. We've already said we're leaving this alone -"*

MeDerra held up a copy of Project Cold Wednesday (well, a version of it), "-the story stops here." He got up, "you see? This is the part where you start to talk about how much fun you had on your little fucking hunt, here. Then - then you say *aw, I wish I could have solved this but it was fun anyway. I hope they find Jane Doe someday* - blah, blah, blah."

He continued, "MeDerra, take a seat. Thank you."

He was him and 'him' was he. It clicked.

"Did you like that story, kid? Can you publish that one? Yeah," (the real) Lattisaw jumped. "That's the shit I want to see." He threw the essay down and walked around the room. "Yep. You're going to publish that one."

"Or, I don't have to publish anything."

They chuckled in concert. "No. That would be pretty convenient, huh? But - no, see, no," he continued. "Let's get this one up and out there. Then we'll talk about the next chapter, yeah?"

The first (not real - maybe) Lattisaw reached into his coat and pulled out a small red notebook. After marking a few things, he walked over to me, opening his phone. Then, my pocket vibrated.

"Phone's on silent, huh? Get that," (the real) Lattisaw spoke. "-eh? Go ahead."

I did need his permission. You know how us men get prideful sometimes and pretend that some tense situations really aren't that bad? Well, this was not that. This was a moment of fear wrapped in another layer of fear. If it wasn't for the red lotus calming me from the corner of the room, I probably would have broken down.

I pulled out my phone and the notification was glowing at me. It pulsated like a coin in a video game. A very important coin, might I add.

"Don't spend it all in one place, kid," said (the real) Lattisaw. "Or, shit… Do what you want. Stay by the phone."

They hurried themselves towards the exit like impatient passengers on a flight just after landing (why do we do that?). My eyes were wide as arcade coins, the kind that are only for show and are too big to use.

THE OTHER BLUE

"I can't accept this."

The red lotus let out a shriek and clamored at her neck. I believe it was air that she was searching for. She scratched and gasped as loud as a geyser. The men didn't say a word. It's almost as if I became invisible.

"Yo! Did you hear me? I can't accept this shit-"

The (not real) Lattisaw stopped and turned to me, "you can and you will. We'll be in touch."

They left no room for conversation. I stood there stunned as the red lotus was choking on air.

24 THE MONEY MINDSET II

Deja cried through the night, as consistent as a TV you fell asleep on. Just noise in the background all night. I shouldn't say the background because I was very much present with her. But, I couldn't stop her from crying and as a parent, I got it. Made sense. It did feel good.

"I jus-, like, what is happening, Austin," she whined in my arms, "how-"

"Shhh, shhh."

"Five million. I cannot-," she continued to whine. "-what did you do? Jesus, what did you write?"

She wanted me to explain it all again. We had been doing this charade for a few hours at that point. I was glad to see her so relieved. Life is just different when you don't have to worry about where your next meal is coming from - even if it is only for a minute. There's something unrelentingly peaceful about financial security. I'm not a scientist (well, I guess I am of sorts but not right now), but I wouldn't be surprised if there was a connection between financial stability and those endorphins. That's what I think was causing my wife to lose her shit. For me, it was different. I felt stable but I also felt guilty. That's what was really on my mind.

"Baby, I- Well, it's not really what I wrote," I nudged her off of me for a second, *"I think they paid me so I wouldn't write anymore-"*

"What's that? What do you mean?" she asked.

The guilt for accepting the money couldn't outweigh the guilt of just now telling my wife what was going on.

"- we've been working on something and I think we were getting too close - to like, something we weren't supposed to know about." I continued, *"it started a few months back. I had to go down Galloway... Listen, the morgue called me to I.D a body-"*

She spiked, "to I.D a body? Austin, what? What the hell?" Those beautiful hands leapt onto her mouth.

"-Listen, just listen. It looked like Sid Garner. The dead girl... It was a mistake. For whatever reason, I was listed as next to kin. I didn't even know the girl. Never seen her before. Two detectives come in, ask me questions, and they're all like, it's a mistake - rah, rah, rah. I try to let it go and can't, so - I end up asking [redacted] about it and we just started digging-"

She grabbed a puzzle piece, "ah! That's what you all were talking about."

"Yeah. Probably. And you know I was writing about it all and that's what they bought. Said they would publish it."

She asked, "who?"

"Those detective guys."

Deja fell back into the bed as some tears dried up and I could tell she felt a little less rich. Still rich, but not rich as hell.

> *"I didn't want it and I should have told you the whole story the other night, or whenever that was - ...That's why things were kind of weird at the hospital because well, you see what I was dealing with. I ain't even want it to get like that - still don't know how we got here."*

"Well," she rolled over into my eyes, "whatever you wrote must have been damned-good."

She laughed with smiling tears. My wife was back and through all the chaos, I recognized it in that specific moment. Like, her comment had me smiling from ear to ear.

"The good thing is, we've already got some coins together. Could use more," she laughed. "-But, we don't need this. Not like this. You were right."

I loved that it didn't hurt her to say that because we actually really needed it. It really told me who wins the war between money and love when it comes to Deja. It all made sense. She wasn't crying a millionaire's happy tears anymore, but she was smiling a mother's grin and a wife's glow. We were already millionaires in spirit.

The moment she fell asleep, I slid her off of me. Morning was just a few seconds away.

***

I didn't have a way to get in touch with those guys but I was going to call the bank and alert the transaction, hopefully reverse it. The morning's notifications

259

overwhelmed my phone and many of the headlines were
dominated with some sort of Jane Doe story. That's when I
knew it was too late. By lunch time, I had outlets chasing me
for a comment. Deja was crying even louder because now
she was an ill-legitimate millionaire and possibly an illegal
one. Or, at least her husband was, for sure. Things had gotten
really serious in a matter of a few hours.

"Looks like our Jane Doe is the story now," Apple
Pie said as I answered the phone.

I just held it. Honestly, I felt empty. I felt really worried.

"You know that's my story."

She spiked, "wait - what? All of this is coming from
you?"

"I mean, not really but kind of. Can you meet?"

I could hear the worry in her tone, "Yeah. Let's meet
at -"

"Aht, aht," I interrupted, *"just meet me where it started.
The usual."*

She responded, "oh, ok…"

25 THE MONEY MINDSET III

She was sitting in the corner with a golden hood on, in front of the StarFox game. I knew it was her. I smiled. She's one of my greatest gifts from Echodale.

"They must be good."

Her eyes were buried in fries.

"Sit down, boy," she said to me.

It was a joyous beat in the middle of a sad song. The tenors cried with laughter. Just as they did when we first met. I slid her a thick envelope. She picked it up and slammed it down.

She fired, "Austin. What is this about?"

"Well, part of it is to say thank you. You know, for being there."

She looked confused, "ok... I don't need your money, Austin. Where did you even get all of this? Weren't you just talking about your coins?"

"It's not mine."

Can you imagine what she did next? You know her now. You know her witt and that uncanny ability to know everything. Believe it or not, I didn't have to explain much of anything at that point. She thumbed through the money one time before throwing it back on the table.

"You know I can't accept that… And you shouldn't either," she said.

Her eyes wanted me in a prison that her heart had the key to. I wore shame like a woolskin coat in a California summer. She wouldn't subscribe to the idea that since the story had already broken, we were simply too late. I didn't know what else to say.

"They threatened me. I'm a father."

I left her room to realize that she is a mother.

When she did, she said, "I've 'gotta go."

I reached in my soul and let out all of its air as I watched her walk down the stairs. There was so much more to share with her about it all but she didn't want to hear it. I already felt guilty for bringing her into this mess. I had to let her leave and deal with the pain of it all.

***

Mark brought over some more fries and I ended up burying my eyes in them, too. I pulled out my phone and started scrolling around the Jane Doe topic. The article had been a bombshell discovery and people were amazed to see my name on it. I could tell that some of the comments were very proud and excited for me. They had to have been worried about me after the last few years of headlines. It may not have been basketball but it was certainly another big story with my name on it. This time it had Impact's name on it, too.

"Ah, that wave came crashing in, eh?" a shadowy voice appeared.

I looked up and it was Bingo. That son-of-a-bitch.

"Bingo! Wassup, sir?"

He threw his stubby leg under the table and kept the other one in the aisle. What a smile.

"Austin, hey. I see that face, son," Bingo pointed.

"Yeah?"

He continued, "hell yeah. You've got that 'new-dad' look. - Trying to understand it all, huh?"

"I mean, you can say that. Definitely."

"You know," he continued, "it's the protective thing that really fucks us. We want to stand guard, you know? No matter what 'she cost' there."

Also, I just want to share that he snuck two fries in his mouth during his statement. Two of my fries, by the way. It was only a nod from me. I could have chosen some words and a tone but the best I could do is a nod. I did agree and I did want more.

"Mmmm," he cleared his throat (of those stolen fries - the nerve), "but- [smack, smack] You'see, some of those costs just got to be paid. Lighten up."

He stared into my eyes and warmed me. It was the least he could do after stealing my precious food. All jokes aside, he shared those words with me at the most perfect time. My exhausted soul appreciated it. The red lotus gently massaged my back when he said it. Her hands were as warm as muffins and as soothing as rich chocolate chips.

***

I walked down the stairs, drunk on salt, stumbling through the doors of curiosity.

"Austin," a voice called out. "Can we have a moment?"

It was the two Lattisaws and one was brandishing a weapon. Think of it as a shock collar on a small dog. It was a little threat. Chihuahua-sized. We stretched out in their cruiser.

"We need to make sure this doesn't get out," one of them turned to me with a small stack of papers. Then he handed me the pen, "please?"

They were NDA's without a seal or stamp. Just pages of wordy agreements pledging myself to secrecy about our Blue Jane Doe and dealings with those two bozos.

"Oh, and if you fuck us on this, we'll still win. And, your family will pay," he affirmed.

THE OTHER BLUE

"You leave my family out of this."

He replied, "protect them. Get out."

If you're thinking they explained anything, they didn't. Stop looking for it. Hell, it happened thousands of years ago and I finally just stopped looking for them to explain anything myself. It seemed like after their jig was up, they just laid down the law and left. They didn't tell and I didn't ask, a charade you get used to when dealing with the unreasonable. I think you just try to limit dealing with them, at some point. I signed the papers.

***

It was a silent drive home for me. I didn't really like to mess with Deja's radio anyway but I also needed the quiet. Just to process my new life. It was one of those mental-tunnels that lives outside of the realms of time. It felt like I got home in 3 seconds, or so, even though the trip was really like 20 minutes. Deja was still bright and glowy. I walked in and she was on the floor playing with the twins. She looked up at me in slow motion, harps played when she smiled and adjusted her hair. Then she turned back to the twins. I closed the door as the red lotus walked in.

"Jesus."

Deja looked up, "what's wrong, hon?"

"All this mail."

I began sorting through pieces and throwing out those god-forbidden (and unwarranted) carry out menus from local restaurants. We'd also been getting a lot of business mail from people looking to connect with Impact. But we got one piece of mail that I still have right now. Look in the chest under my bed and grab that envelope with the World Trade Center stamps and blue ink. It's from Mangold.

Thank you.

***

So, he wanted me to essentially forget the other letter and start fresh with this one (as if that were possible). All that he wanted me to do was read his final poem before being put to death. Apparently, that's all he ever wanted. He said he would have read it to me. It reads:

> *In the shadows, we fall victim to fear. We are no longer the axis, but the spinning globe. We used to watch the stars go round and round but we can't see them from here anymore. Now, we just follow the axis and move where it says go. Unless we become the axis. Being the axis is key.*

It was a beautiful piece of advice, I'd thought. Sure, it was weird because of my tie to the author but if feeling something while digesting poetry is the key to appreciating it, then this was that. I folded it up and put it on my nightstand. I had read it 4 times by then. It felt good reading it, really.

***

My email was flooded with Jane Doe-story appreciation and speculations. Some thought I was describing their sister and others thought I was making it all up. I was even asked to sit with a sketch artist and see if they could piece together her features. It was too late though because Echodale Police began releasing their 'sketches' but none of them looked like her, to me. I was struggling to trust everything around me. It was a very confusing time. I couldn't hold myself from being honest about it. When people asked what I thought of the sketch, I told them it wasn't who I remembered. The features weren't even right. It felt intentional and it bothered me. That's when the guilt started strangling me again. The red lotus was coughing and shit.

***

"[Redacted]? Have you seen Detective [redacted]?"

The clerk at EPD replied, "Oh, [redacted]? She just left not too long ago."

"Do you know what time she'll be coming back?"

She smiled, "she won't be. New assignment, hon."

My heart farted.

"Uh, ok. We-ll, uh... Where can I find her?"

"Private assignment," she affirmed into my eyes. As stoic as Apple Pie would. They must grow fields of these women. "Listen, can I help you with something? You'guys had a case?"

I tapped the desk and walked away. That meeting at StarStrike was the last time I would ever see Apple Pie. We've spoken since then but never physically connected. She really did get a new assignment but at that time, I thought she was just trying to run away from me and my troubled world. If I tell you anymore about her new gig, I'll have to kill you.

***

Anyways, I walked out of that EPD Station for the last time. I was hoping that she could help me sort out this guilt in a legal and safe way. She's perfect for that intersection, you know? But that wasn't an option. That's how I ended up sitting in the Karlston Station Cafe', across from Sid Garner. She was wearing a black fur hat and pitch-black shades.

She was a sweet girl but very forward. We talked about Perry and the marriage that neither of them wanted to admit existed. It was all small talk. I heard that is necessary in some arenas. Her smile seemed permanent and her nerves seemed stable. Two odd characteristics of a girl who's sister was missing.

> "So, that friend of yours said you wanted to meet with me about something," Sid spoke. "-What's going on?"

> *"I couldn't stop thinking about you after seeing you at the Gold Mics."*

She began to look frantic.

> *"No, no… Sorry, I mean like, because you looked really familiar. And-"*

> She laughed, "Of course, I'm your teammate's ex-wife. Your very famous teammate." If those eyes could talk they'd be like - '*duh*'.

268

"No but like, more familiar than that. If that makes sense. It was your sister."

She gulped, "Hmph? Pressie? You've seen her."

I didn't know how to tell her where I thought I had seen her. It wouldn't make sense. None of this does, you know? We just stared at each other for hours until finally her face began to speak. A frantic wave flushed her and was replaced with an odd stoicism. She adjusted the bang over her left eye. Her phone rang on the table.

"You should grab that for me. I think it's for you," she said without looking up at me.

Her face was buried in one of those small drink menus, "go on, now. Please."

"He-llo?"

The voice replied, "Austin, I thought we could trust you."

I leaned back in the chair and looked around the busy station. My lips didn't make a sound.

"Oh, looking for me? I'm to your left. Right in front of the steps," he continued, "I thought we could trust you."

"I don't want the money anymore. I just wanted to help this family and get out of this mess."

He affirmed, "well, now you know that she knows. We are not animals - and, we are not… murderers. We don't want to be."

I'm sure he could see my face. I'm sure he could feel my expression.

"Need I remind you that you've inked a contract swearing you'll keep your mouth shut. The money is not even a small concern for us," he continued. It fell silent. "I'm going to have to ask you and your family to leave town, quickly."

"Hello?"

As you can imagine, the call dropped. I watched the two men climb that big staircase. They looked back at us sitting at the table.

"Did they tell you to leave town?" Sid asked without raising her eyes.

"Yes."

"Do it," she continued, "please."

I looked over at the red lotus standing a few feet behind her. She was nodding her head and urging me to come in her direction. That's when I stood up, slid my chair under the table, and gathered myself without saying a word until just before I walked away.

THE OTHER BLUE

"Perry'know about this?"

She replied, "no. He doesn't."

She never looked up. I walked out of the cafe with the red lotus in my arms.

***

Apple Pie's phone was going straight to voicemail. I wish I still had that phone so you could see how many texts I sent her. She never responded to a single character. That number never called again.

Deja whispered into the family room, "-you've got another piece of mail. Up there."

I got up slowly as she exited the room without bidding me farewell. Of course the letter was from Dale Mangold, speaking to me from the other side. I shook my head. It was written on looseleaf paper in blue ink and was pressed like khakis fresh from the cleaners. Oh, it was very dramatic. It didn't greet me and it didn't wish me "all the bests", it was simply this collection of numbers and his signature:

1, 32, 55, 51, 23, 34, 129, 86, 122, 128, 215, 83.

I threw it in the trash. Like, a literal throw with some force. Can't tell you why it frustrated me so much, I think I just wanted to get to the point of all of it. But then it hit me. Those numbers had to mean something, you know? Mangold was psycho but he wasn't a fool. I had grown to understand that he was a very smart guy, just an asshole. Surely you know someone like that. Or, maybe it's you…?

***

The balled-up letter was screaming my name from the trash bin. Other than that, it was silent in the apartment. Deja and the twins must have fallen asleep or she may have been reading. Either way, it was time for me to end all of this.

I un-crumpled the paper and tried to hand-iron it on the coffee table. There were too many numbers to be a combination to a lock, or safe. I thought that was too many numbers for the lottery, too. I added them up and did all sorts of mathematical gymnastics with those damned numbers. I spelled them out to see if there was anything in the words; nope.

Have you figured it out yet? My mind was blown when I did.

***

After a few hours, I took those numbers and paired it with the previous letter from Mangold. I had stuck with the idea of it being a combination but maybe not to a lock. My eyes bounced between those two papers for what felt like eternity. As if they were two retardant lily pads floating down a stream of lava. It took me a few days but I got a little closer.

One morning, I was walking around the kitchen, trying to calm down my crying twins. Deja was a few days away from her return to the news and she was out running errands. That was an exciting time for her, she loved it. James and Germany didn't like it so much, though. I won't say they hated me but I didn't have those boobs that the three of us enjoyed. Nor did I have that sultry voice that loved to hum them to sleep. All I had was love. Oh, and curiosity. It took them some time but they learned to rest on what I was working with. But that day in particular? Hell no. Those kids were all over the place. That's how I knew they would end up being my rambunctious two.

So, I cheated. I put a little something-something in their bottles and watched them drift into the land of sleepy babies. I had to, man. I think I had figured out Mangold's message and I couldn't let those crying infants (who I love dearly - even now) ruin my brain power. I closed the door and gave them some peace (not that they needed it because they were out cold - mommy never knew). The next few minutes went something like this: letter, letter, letter, letter, first sentence, letter, greeting, letter, first paragraph, letter - and so on. Then it happened: letter, poem, letter, poem. I took those numbers from the letter and lined them up with that beautiful poem from my best friend's murderer.

I wrote them out. Hand me that paper over there - like this:

1

32

55

51

23

34

129

86

122

128

215

83

Right? Real nice and neat. I was hunched over the coffee table with my legs wide open and my chain dangling just below my chin. Mrs. Dortch's cat was scratching the wall. Then, I went through the poem and lined those numbers up with their coinciding letter. It looked something like this:

1 - "I"
32 - "W"
55 - "T"
51 - "S"
23 - "T"
34 - "A"
129 - "R"
86 - "E"
122 - "M"
128 - "E"
215 - "K"
83 - "H"

I almost lied to you. I was thinking about it. You know, to fluff my intelligence a little bit. But you wouldn't be sitting right here if you didn't value me already so I'll be honest. I stared at those numbers and letters for a few hours. I'm sure you figured it out already because you're smart. Deja was resting on my chest and the twins were sleeping in their bassinets.

"Baby," I tapped her, "-let me up, I'll be back."

She was half asleep and wasn't even coherent enough to care. It hit me though.

26 THE SCARZGARD

You remember what I told you yesterday? About how Madame Gist spoke of a mysterious group named "MERK". They were tied into Pettigrew and his gang on the Chariot. Her words hit me like a 3 ton bowling ball while I was laying in bed. I just didn't think it was a coincidence that those letters lined up perfectly. Sure, it could have been something else but do you really think that? You know what they say about coinkydinks. All of this is in Project Cold Wednesday (the actual version) and that's pretty much how it happened. But, what did it all mean?

***

"Honey?" Deja yawned over my shoulder. "Can we just let the cat in?"

It was a really good idea. That damned cat just wanted to be loved and I was in such a good mood, I didn't care. Deja opened the door and Mrs. Dortch's cat scurried into the corner of the kitchen and I feel like it's still there now. I don't even remember Dortch asking about it. The red lotus came and sat next to me. Deja slept-walk back to her lair (it's her world, I just lived in it). I looked at the lotus in her badass red leather body suit covered in a red trench coat made of wool. She crossed her legs and showed off those high heels that I like. The ones with the thick platform and pointy heel - 7 inches, baby. Red lotus was ready and I was too. In fact, I was because she was. If you know her then you'll understand.

I fell into her arms and melted into the solitude of the room. Like ice in a boiling pot of water, I rested on brain

275

power and pride. I was damned proud of that. It was weird because he surely killed my best friend (and plead guilty to all charges), but I felt like I had heard Mangold's message from the other side. Now it was time to make something out of it.

***

We met at a pool in the Scarzgard Hotel in downtown Echodale. She waded in the pool with weeping eyes while Derry covered his face with the day's paper poolside. It was loud and it was crowded but we huddled in the corner of the pool, covered by the warm bodies around us and as blended in as printer paper in the snow.

"I don't want to do this," she pleaded.

"- Then, why are we here? It's for your sister, isn't it?"

Sid was silent but her emotional eyes said it all. She wiped her face from the splashing surface of the pool.

"-Huh?"

She replied, "-yes. For Pressie. I miss her."

Screaming kids splashed around us. Their parents were nowhere to be found.

"What am I doing?" she asked herself aloud.

"You're being human. Whatever happened-"

She interrupted, "I thought she was missing too."

Her chilled emotion grew stale and she submerged herself underwater for a refresh before reappearing like a supermodel in Mexico.

"But, she wasn't," she said. "She was dead."

It was her stare that was the most frightening of her statements. Actually, it was the emotional ping-pong that she was able to play with ease. Without a whimper or a single drop of sweat.

"I'm numb, Austin. Very numb. I want to feel. Well. I guess, I never anticipated any of this shit," she swam around me. "But what do you do? These guys follow me everywhere and trap me. Threaten me."

"Those cop guys?"

She chuckled, "they're not police. I don't know what the hell they are but they're not cops." "So, you saw my sister's body huh?"

"I don't know."

"Yeah, you did. Had to," she affirmed before falling back into the water, floating like a dead rose in the pond.

Her breasts reminded me of her sister's. My heart was on fire and my soul was on ice. I dropped my head under the water, man, trying to get some air or something. I know that doesn't make sense but I was an emotional wreck with twins and a beautiful wife at home. For whatever reason, I heard the grim reaper playing an out-of-tune violin. Very faint sound but loud enough to lull my heart into a daze of fear and wonder.

"Lefthand," Derry said over my shoulder as I resurfaced, "we- we should go."

His eyes pointed towards the main entrance. The two Lattisaws were standing there in speedos and flip flops. I could smell the musky cologne from over here. Even right now, decades later, I can still smell that shit.

"Yeah, we should."

Sid Garner was gone.

Derry spoke, "it's about being calm, lefthand. Always about being calm."

I dried off as a normal person would and we put on our clothes poolside.

He followed, "now, let's calmly leave, shall we?"

***

We cleared the side entrance and walked behind the lobby. By the time we came around the side (trying to get to the hotel doors), they were standing on the other side of the pool's entrance. Still in speedos. Yes, standing in the lobby in speedos.

"Change of plans."

I led us down the hall (beautiful, by the way - purple carpet, gold lamp-posts, mood lighting) of the first floor rooms, to the plaza elevators. We were as calm as sand in the desert. On the outside, at least. Inside? I was ready to shit my pants but that's our little secret.

"I guess they were exactly how you described, lefthand," Derry said to me as we stood in the elevator.

"I guess so."

He laughed, "'Atta boy."

"Mr. Arrington," a bold voice cornered us as the elevator doors opened. "Sir," he continued to Derry before boarding the elevator and closing the door. "What I can't understand is why you two are at the Scarzgard of all places?"

He pushed the second floor button and turned a key in a latch hidden next to the buttons. You probably want me to describe the guy, but I can't. He had one of those distinctive looks that seemed to change the more you looked at him, you know? He was tall. I guess that's a description. Dark skin, that too.

***

"Please," he led us off of the elevator.

It was a hall of smoke-tint glass and white lights. Some were massive rooms and others were hotel administrative holdings. Derry smiled at me. Never shaken or stirred, always present. The end of the hall led to two flights of stairs leading down to an unrecognizable part of the Scarzgard campus. It was dim-lit and antique. The music was the loudest thing in the room. Until he spoke.

> "Hmph," **he** gulped as we shuffled down the stairs. "Let's just clear the air and get things straight, eh? Yeah? Yeah."

As the view became clearer, the first I saw was the red lotus duct-taped in the corner with drowning eyes. Her red dress was without saturation. It was moments away from gray. She was screaming but I couldn't hear her. I could feel it, though.

> So, he says to me, "you guys have nailed this thing and you won't leave it the fuck alone. Yeah? I wouldn't either. Sometimes you need a little motivation."

It was Tom Force.

> "- You fucked me in Paradise and here you are, fucking me again. And, Derry? Why are you here, mate? Where's your boat, huh? Why'd you give it up," he said walking around the room.

We stood calm. This was before Tommy took over Vaden and all that other shit his family owns now. He was still a big player in the media game back then, though.

"Listen, I'll just end this little train here. You guys know it wasn't me. It happened, but it wasn't me. Well… I know who it was and how it happened but yeah, not me," he affirmed. "You just keep snoopin'. Eh? You shouldn't follow every scent, you know? Some things get you killed…Like your friend. Well, both of your friends."

We said nothing. There was nothing to be said. The only thing I was thinking about saying was 'goodbye' to Deja and the twins.

"I'll let you in on this part. She wouldn't stop snooping either," he whispered to the room.

"Listen, I just had twins, man. He's just retired. We shouldn't have-"

He interrupted, "wait, no, no, no. I'm not 'gonna hurt you. None of us will."

I put my hands down, slow, like honey sliding down a sand dune.

"So, we can leave then?"

"Well, not quite. See, the problem is that you're still here. In Echodale. And…then, my guys ask me about that and they get upset at **me**. Because we had asked you to leave us and here you are," he replied.

"I've got a family, I can't just up and leave. It takes -"

He interrupted, "motivation, yes. I know I know. That's what we're meeting about tonight, see. No one wants to hurt you, see. Or, your family. We've just had ourselves a bit of an accident and you're tangled right on up in there. I mean, is it money? If you need some more, we can do that."

I shook my head but my eyes stayed focused on the red lotus. My heart was crying for my lady.

"Your phone's about to ring," he continued.

It did, I answered.

The voice said, "Austin, yes! Yes! Yes!"

"Sh-, shade? Whoa-"

"You got it, bud. Whatever you need. It's done -," he replied.

"Say ok," Tommy whispered to me.

He gestured his hand as if I was speaking too long during an engagement.

"Ok, I'll just - have to call you back… Dunno what's going on."

The mad man walked us over to this beautiful conference room table. We sat down as if we were signing on a house. I wasn't intimidated by this guy anymore. Something about the last few moments (which is all everything ever is) softened his tough appeal to me. We needed to talk.

"What the hell was that?"

He leaned back in his chair, "that was your old and new boss. You're back at RUMBLE until we can get you out of town."

"Hell no! What is this - "

The man replied, "it's survival. Listen, we aren't evil - we, we don't kill, see. But ending your life is a lot easier than you…probably believe. A lot easier, nowadays. - We won't kill you but we will end your life, see?"

He shuffled some things around the table, "-job, Deja's job… Accounts froz'd. Or, frozen. Credit. Just - Please, just work with us on this. I understand what you need and I can work with you. Want to…work with you. We'just need to work together on this. Ok?"

No words. Derry had none either.

"12 months. The both of you… Then I can't help after that, I'm trying," he continued. "You'll do th'radio while you're here, keep you busy and… we'll watch, see."

"Sounds like -"

He interrupted, "you don't really have a choice, son. I mean, you don't. Let's just work together and end this... You can go take care of those twins, take th'money. Do what you'need. Build that celebrity'whatever. It was an accident, see. All of this- and I just have to keep you out of things."

***

That's what he said. I remember when I finally started to share about that whole ordeal, people were saying that they didn't believe me. Then, when they started to put the pieces together, they had to. What would you have done?

I never agreed to anything. There weren't enough words in the English language to even try and develop a response to his command. It was all about that gyal, the red lotus. It was about those eyes - how they yearned. They loved making sweet music with Deja's. They would sing and dance together. They were always worth fighting for, always worth protecting.

***

She was mad for quite some time. I never told Deja about that night at Scarzgard.

"The Jane Doe will be identified in the morning," he said as we climbed the stairs (poor Derry was struggling).

"I know nothing about it."

27 Family is the Only Truth

The more levels you climb, the more pain you know. We just accumulate more moments and increase the risk of losing them. You know the stakes have been high for me since I was at State. It's just been responsibility after responsibility, piling itself on as I've achieved. At the end of every row of cheering fans is the unimpressed coach introducing you to more pain. It leads to progress of some sort (in most cases), but it's just a cycle.

That's what I was thinking about as the lo-fi beats intertwined with the dim lights of our apartment bedroom. Deja was out in the front room with the twins and I had some time alone. Just me and the red lotus.

I thanked her for giving me something to fight for and teaching me patience; learning to live with her has been a journey in itself. One that has only one result; growth. I discovered what makes her smile. I found that keeping her quiet is the safest way to navigate my life and responsibilities. I've learned to live with her.

***

I was all alone that night. I figured the less time that I spent with Deja, the less inclined I was to tell her what had taken place at Scarzgard. She was really happy, you know? We saw it every day when she did her reports. The station was so grateful to have her back, I think the city was, actually. Her shine was something that everyone looked forward to. She was really delicate with Echodale. Then, she was excited to hear me back on the radio and how successful things had become after that whole ordeal.

That first version of PCW is still one of the most shared online-documents, today. I think people have a hard time believing what was happening around them, hiding in plain sight. It's hard to read that first one and then pick up mine.

***

That man was right, the Jane Doe was identified that next morning. It was Roya "Pressie" Garner, sister of philanthropist, media-maven, influencer (but mostly known for being the ex-wife of Armonti Perry), Sid Garner. They ran DNA of Roya's stuff back in Seattle and matched it with DNA from the Jane Doe. Of course, she had been cremated already so everyone kind of had to take the official's word for it. That's why no one asked questions, you know? Her death was a mystery until it wasn't even a memory. Well, until I started talking. It's still crazy thinking about how quickly people moved on from things and just stopped caring.

***

We started building the house in Montana Bay. Everything came together. Merk got what it wanted and so did we. With all of the money Impact had made (wink wink), it really did make sense to get what we needed in life. A humble apartment with an old lady next door and refugee cats didn't add up anymore.

Sid seemed like such a bitch but she ended up becoming a sweetheart. That's how I knew that whatever happened really was an accident. I believed them. Still do. I don't think today is the day for that one but I'll tell you how all of that unfolded. Right now, I'd like to lay back and think about my family.

Like I did that night in Echodale.

EPILOGUE

Austin's eyes followed the young Psychiatrist out of the room. He could see the goosebumps on his arms. The room rocked from his trembling. We digest some stories about as smooth as a raw steak. Mr. Arrington wasn't exactly sure about what made it difficult. *Was it the murder? Was it the initial investment in ImpactComm? Did Rose not know how important an initial investment is?*

Austin's life has proven to be quite the tale. He's been an inspiration to so many at nearly every stage of his long life. Now that the sun is setting, it's pure art putting the pieces of his life together, creating one massive painting. All of the shocking details coupled with the many moments that strained his undying love for his wife. We see successful people but don't know what those souls have been through.

> "Kid," Mr. Arrington scratched as Professor Rose put on his coat. "Tomorrow we will smile and we will cry."

Professor Rose nodded. The corners of his eyes sank like wet paper. Austin climbed out of his seat and hugged Professor Rose as if he was returning home from war. He rubbed his back and rested his head on his shoulders. He mumbled something but no one heard him, not even Professor Rose.

> "Oh, this…Look! Lefthand. This," Austin reached down. "Can't forget this."

"Thank you, sir."

Rose loved baseball caps and he had on a special black one from Maryland State. His wife suggested that he wore it to the session today. Would have been a shame for him to go home without it.

"I'd sign it if it wasn't black, you know," Austin smiled.

Rose flipped it, "well, sir. How's this side?"

That side was much better. The bill of the cap was red underneath with white stitching. Austin autographed it with a sharpie from his desk. He shuffled back over to Rose like a grandfather with his favorite baseball mitt; a gift to his loving grandson.

"See you tomorrow," said the old man.

MEET BRIAN JAMES

THANK YOU.

The true joy of writing (for me) is being able to connect with readers from across the world. Different creeds, colors, backgrounds, fears, and everything. It truly is special to be able to meet other writers and readers. Even more enjoyable being able to share my worlds with you.

I'm like many other writers - these words are where I hide. Your support allows me to be seen, heard, and felt. That's something I never take for granted. I appreciate it with every ounce of blood in my body.

Peace be with you! Soar without fear. Until the next time,

ROADMAP

Are you new to The Man Who Didn't Stop Running series? Maybe you're continuing your journey. No matter where you are, stay up to date with Austin and Deja Arrington.

Follow their journey of eventful love from their college romance days until the end.

Here's your roadmap:

IF: The Other Blue is your first TMWDSR Experience,

then,

READ NEXT: Embers

Made in the USA
Middletown, DE
06 May 2023